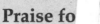

By Kinley MacGregor

Lords of Avalon®
KNIGHT OF DARKNESS
SWORD OF DARKNESS

Brotherhood of the Sword
THE WARRIOR
RETURN OF THE WARRIOR
A DARK CHAMPION
TAMING THE SCOTSMAN
BORN IN SIN
CLAIMING THE HIGHLANDER
MASTER OF DESIRE

Sea Wolves
MASTER OF SEDUCTION
A PIRATE OF HER OWN

KINLEY MACGREGOR

THE WARRIOR

BROTHERHOOD OF THE SWORD

AVON

An Imprint of HarperCollinsPublishers

This is a work of fiction. Names, characters, places, and incidents are products of the author's imagination or are used fictitiously and are not to be construed as real. Any resemblance to actual events, locales, organizations, or persons, living or dead, is entirely coincidental.

AVON BOOKS
An Imprint of HarperCollins*Publishers*
10 East 53rd Street
New York, New York 10022-5299

First Avon Books paperback printing: December 2007

Avon Trademark Reg. U.S. Pat. Off. and in Other Countries, Marca Registrada, Hecho en U.S.A.
HarperCollins® is a registered trademark of HarperCollins Publishers.

Printed in the U.S.A.

10 9 8 7 6 5 4 3 2 1

THE
WARRIOR

BROTHERHOOD OF THE SWORD

Prologue

It was long after dark when Lochlan MacAllister and his brothers, Braden and Sin, sat with the father of their brother Ewan's new wife. The overhead candles had been doused and the hall was illuminated only by the fire in the large fireplace that rested along the right wall.

Its light played against the banners and weapons that decorated the whitewashed walls, dancing strange shapes all around them while they joked and sampled the food that had been left out before the servants had taken their leave of them.

The happy couple had retired hours ago and no one had seen a single sight of Ewan or Nora since.

Not that they expected to.

Indeed, given Lochlan's knowledge of his brother, he fully expected days would go by before either of them showed themselves again.

It was something that made his heart soar.

He was glad happiness had finally come to his brother. Ewan had needed it.

"I can't believe we got Ewan married off before Lochlan," Braden said as he picked at a platter of sliced fruit that was set before him. "We needs be careful, Sin. I think the Second Coming might be upon us. I feel the sudden urge for Confession."

Sin laughed. "Perhaps."

"Have you any more word about the Mac-Kaids?" Nora's father Alexander asked.

Lochlan shook his head. How he wished to find them. And he would. He wouldn't rest until they paid for what they had attempted to do to his family.

"None of my men have found a trace of them," he said to Alexander. "Have yours?"

"Nay."

"That sits ill with me," Sin said. "I have a feeling we haven't heard the last of them."

"Most likely not," Lochlan concurred.

"So what should we do?" Alexander asked. "I've notified my cousin what they've done and he has issued an order of execution for them, but until they're caught . . ."

"There's not much we can do," Braden said.

Sin finished off his tankard of ale and poured more. "Sure there is."

"What?" Braden asked.

"Marry Lochlan off."

Lochlan shoved playfully at Sin's arm. "You're drunk."

"Is he?" a feminine voice asked.

They looked up to see Sin's wife, Caledonia approaching the table.

She moved around the side of the table until she was behind Sin's chair. Looking down at her husband, she gave him a chiding, gentle smile. "I had a feeling my wayward husband was spending far too much time down here."

Sin looked a bit sheepish.

"Come, my lord," she said, taking Sin's hand. "We have a long journey home tomorrow and I promised my brother Jamie that we would be back in time for his birthday."

Sin kissed her hand, then rubbed it against his cheek.

Lochlan was amazed by the gesture that was so alien to Sin. It was good to see his brother so well suited with wife.

Sin was another one he had never expected to see happy. It did him good to know life had finally treated his elder brother kindly.

"Good night gentlemen," Sin said, rising to follow after his wife.

They passed Maggie in the entranceway.

Lochlan smiled as she came forward, eyeing the three of them suspiciously. He remembered a time when he had contemplated her death and had wished many vile things upon her.

Now he was glad he had refrained from the urge to kill her.

"Look lively, Braden," he said to his youngest brother. "'Tis your turn to have your ears boxed."

Braden scoffed, "My sweet Maggie knows better than to box my ear, eh, love?"

There was a saucy sway to her hips as she approached the table. "It depends on if you've done anything to have them boxed for."

She smiled sweetly at Alexander and Lochlan. "Do you mind if I steal him away from you?"

"Not at all," Alexander said.

Braden got up, swept her up in his arms, and headed for the stairs at an almost dead run.

Lochlan watched them leave, his heart light at his brother's antics. No doubt, Maggie would be gifting him with another niece or nephew soon.

"So," Alexander said once they were alone. "Have you any plans to take a bride?"

Lochlan swirled the ale around in his cup as he considered that. In truth, there was no woman in his heart. He doubted if there ever would be. But still, his duty commanded him to take a bride.

There was only so long he could put off that particular responsibility.

"Mayhap one day," he said quietly.

Alexander arched a brow at him. "Aren't you a little old now not to be looking?"

Perhaps he was. But Lochlan had too many things that demanded his time and marrying a woman sight unseen wasn't something he relished.

"To everything there is a season."

Alexander laughed at that.

Footsteps sounded outside the room, followed by the main door opening and closing.

Lochlan and Alexander exchanged puzzled frowns.

It was far too late for company.

An old servant entered the hall with a youth behind him. The boy hadn't quite reached his majority.

Dressed in rags, the boy carried a weathered satchel.

"Forgive me, my lord," the old servant said to Alexander. "The lad said he had news of Lysander."

Alexander motioned the boy to come forward. "Is there a problem?"

The boy hesitated, then shrank back. He looked hesitantly at the servant, then to Lochlan.

"Speak, lad," Alexander said patiently. "No one here will harm you."

Still the boy looked doubtful. "I have word, my lord. This man came to our village and he told me I was to bring this to you."

The boy rushed forward, dropped the satchel on the table, then ran back to a safe distance as if he expected the wrath of hell to fall down upon his young head.

Lochlan frowned at his fearful actions.

Alexander ran his hand over the worn leather. "Is this Lysander's?"

The boy swallowed. "I know not, my lord. I was only told to give it you and to not open it."

By the pallor of the boy's face, Lochlan could surmise the child hadn't listened.

"Who gave you this?" Lochlan asked.

The youth scratched his neck nervously. "He said there was a letter for Lord Alexander inside and . . . and to tell his lordship that next time you should hire yourself someone better than a French knight." The boy was shaking. "Can I go home now, please, my lord?"

Alexander nodded.

The boy shot from the room as if Lucifer's hounds were after him.

Lochlan's frown deepened.

Alexander studied the bag. "How very strange."

"Aye," Lochlan said, leaning forward to look at it as well. "It is indeed."

Alexander opened the satchel and dumped its contents onto the table.

Lochlan stood up the instant he saw the green-and-black plaid that their father had commissioned years ago for his sons. He'd never known anyone other than he and his brothers to have it.

His blood went cold as he stared at it in disbelief.

Alexander opened a small piece of parchment while Lochlan pulled the plaid closer to examine it.

"Canmore," he read aloud, "I don't like being made a fool of by anyone. You can tell the gypsies that they are next on our list. You should have never told the king about us. Had you stayed quiet, your daughter might have lived. Now we'll be coming for her and the rest of the MacAllisters. Guard your backs carefully."

Alexander's hands shook and his face turned dark red with rage. "It's signed Graham Mac-Kaid."

Lochlan barely heard the words. He was too fixated by the initials embroidered in the corner of the tattered and worn plaid.

K.M.
Kieran MacAllister.

But how?

Who would have had his brother's plaid? No one outside of their clan would have access to it.

Seeking more clues, Lochlan unfolded the material and cursed as a disembodied hand fell to the floor.

Alexander's own curse rang out as he saw it and the strange brand that was on the back of the hand.

"So help me," he growled. "I'll kill every one of those bastards for this."

Lochlan found it hard to breathe. Hard to focus. He ran through his mind the man whom he had met briefly. A man he had paid all too little attention to.

"Who was Lysander?" he asked Alexander.

"I don't know to be honest. I found him in France about five years ago when I went to visit a friend. He had just come back from Outremer and refused to speak of it."

"And this plaid?"

Alexander shrugged. "It was wrapped around him when he asked for work. Does it mean something to you?"

It meant more to him than his own life. "Did he say how he came by it?"

He shook his head. "I only know it was very dear to him. My wife's maid tried to take it from him once to clean it and he almost tore her arm for the trouble. He was rather feral in the early days of his employment."

Alexander retrieved the hand and went to find the priest to dispose of it.

Lochlan ran the monogrammed corner of the plaid through his long fingers as he stared at the initials his mother had placed there.

How had a Frenchman found Kieran's plaid?

None of the brothers had ever journeyed farther than England except for Sin and Sin had never taken a plaid with him.

If not for the initials, he might think that perhaps the weaver had created more of the design and sold it.

But those initials matched the one for his plaid, Braden's, and Ewan's.

Nay, this was Kieran's. He knew it. There was no doubt in his mind that it was his brother's and by the looks of it, it was quite old.

A souvenir of Outremer.

Which meant that Kieran hadn't died that day when he'd gone out to the loch on his own.

For some unknown reason, his brother had faked his own death, then left Scotland.

But why?

Why would Kieran not send word to them? Why would he allow them to believe he was dead all these years?

Lochlan sat down as the news sank in.

No doubt the MacKaids had found the plaid after they killed Lysander and had sent it back to them.

They would have known exactly who this belonged to and what it meant.

Lochlan drained his ale in one gulp.

Somewhere out there, Kieran MacAllister might still be alive.

And God have mercy on his brother should he ever find him.

Chapter 1

Eight months later

Catarina ground her teeth as she pressed her thumb tight to her palm in an effort to pull her hand free of the rope that held her in place. Sweat was dripping down from her brow, making her nose itch, but she didn't dare swipe at it. Time was too precious for that.

Any moment her kidnappers would return.

How she despised them for their deeds and wished a festering pox on every part of their bodies, especially that part which men valued most.

The coarse rope burned against her skin, chafing it as she worked to free herself. Not that she cared. All that mattered was her freedom. And when she had it, she would make all of them pay for taking her from the ones she loved. How dare they!

She snatched her hand again and again against the prickly rope, trying to free it. Then she dipped her head in an effort to loosen the massive knot with her teeth. Instead of loosening the knot, it felt more like she was only loosening her teeth. Cursing, she closed her eyes and prayed as she tugged against the rope with all of her might.

She felt the skin breaking as the hemp scratched her flesh. Even so, she didn't let up and in one painful slip, her hand came free.

If she were the crying type, Cat would have wept in relief, but tears had been something she'd forsaken years ago. Wiping her brow finally, she took a deep breath, then blew air across her hand to alleviate some of the throbbing as she looked about the sparse room for a weapon.

There was nothing . . .

Except the fire. She narrowed her gaze on the burning logs as an idea occurred to her. Reaching beneath her gown, she tore at her chemise until she had enough of it to pad her hands before she reached into the fire.

"Think you she's ready to give us no more trouble?"

Her heart leapt at the sound of men approaching her room. Stepping back from the makeshift hearth, she gripped the limb tightly in both hands. She moved to stand behind the door where they wouldn't be able to see her until after it was too late.

"Any more trouble from her and I say we thrash her soundly, orders or no orders."

"Good luck at that. My eye still throbs from its last encounter with her fist. I swear the bitch hits like a man."

They swung open the door.

Cat held her breath until they were inside the room with her. Her gaze never wavering, she swung with the whole of her strength against the second man's head.

He yelped, then fell against the first. Her heart hammering, she lobbed the limb against the first man, clubbing him thrice, then grabbed her skirts and ran as swiftly as she could.

She ducked out of the tack room and ran for the stable's opening. The men called out for her to stop, but she refused.

Nothing short of death would make her surrender to them.

Cat hesitated outside as she saw the number of people in the small village. Many turned to stare at her as she ran for a saddled horse at the edge of town. To steal such would mean her head if she were caught. But truthfully she'd rather die than meet the future those men would carry her off to.

"Stop her!" one of the men shouted. "Twenty gold francs to whoever catches her."

Cat winced as the crowd looked on her with new interest. Twenty francs was a fortune. A large burly man stepped in front of her. She pulled up short, then kicked him as hard as she could between his legs. He doubled over, but before she could maneuver past him, another man caught her from behind.

She rammed her head back to slam it into his face. He cursed as she spun from his hands, her own skull aching from the blow. Another tried to capture her. She ran her shoulder into his middle and shoved him back, causing him to fall into the dirt.

But before she could straighten, someone else ran at her and knocked her to the ground, flat on her back. She gasped as the breath left her lungs. Still, she wasn't defeated. Rolling over, she shot to her feet only to be knocked down again.

Desperate, she scrambled on the ground, trying to escape only to find her way blocked by a pair of scuffed black leather boots. She glared at them with hatred burning deep inside her.

Nay!

Refusing to cower, she looked up defiantly at the man blocking her path, then gaped at the sight of the face that met her eyes.

It couldn't be . . .

Time stopped as she met the crystal blue gaze of a man she'd never thought to see again. The last time they'd met, he'd been immaculately coifed. Regal and stern. He'd seemed larger than life, but that vision paled to how he appeared this day.

Now he looked rugged and powerful. Dangerous. Determined and feral. His golden blond hair was windblown and his cheeks dusted with several days' growth of beard. And there was no missing the lethal chill in his eyes as he took in her predicament.

"Are you injured, lass?" Lochlan asked in that deep Scottish brogue before he held one large, strong hand out to her.

Cat could do nothing more than shake her head as she reached for his hand. To her relief, he pulled her to her feet, then placed himself between her and her pursuers.

She couldn't believe her luck as she brushed at the dirt on her gown. Nor could she believe Lochlan would be willing to protect her when no one else had stepped forward.

As her captors neared, Lochlan pulled his sword from its sheath.

"Stand down," the largest guard sneered at him, not knowing that this was one of the most powerful lairds in Scotland. "This be the king's business."

Lochlan scoffed at the man's commanding tone. "King's business, my arse. I don't see the man here and if you have issue with the woman, then you have issue with me."

Cat smiled for the first time in days. She couldn't believe someone was finally taking up for her . . . and it was Lochlan MacAllister no less. He was nothing if not a man who lived his entire life by the rules. She'd never dreamed he would protect her like this.

The shorter guard took a step forward.

Lochlan swung the sword around his body, preparing to engage him.

The man must have come to his senses as he saw Lochlan's obvious skill. He stepped back to a safer distance. "We are under royal orders to deliver her to Paris."

Lochlan glanced at her over his shoulder. "Do you want to go to Paris, Catarina?"

"Not on their lives."

He tsked at her guards. "Well now, the lady has spoken. If you truly have a royal decree, lad, I suggest you show it to me. Otherwise, step back and step down, or you'll be sitting on steel marks for the rest of your life."

A tic worked in the guard's jaw. "You're making a deadly err."

"Then you can play a giddy tune over me grave." Lochlan gave a sharp whistle.

A tall gray horse neighed before it galloped over to him. Lochlan swung himself onto the saddle before he held his hand out to her while keeping his sword angled toward the men.

Cat took his hand and allowed him to pull her up behind him before he spurred his horse into a dead run. Wrapping her arms around his lean waist, she squeezed him tightly in gratitude. If not for the fact she hated the very air this man breathed, she'd kiss him for what he'd done for her.

"Thank you," she said in his ear.

Lochlan didn't speak as he looked behind him to see that the other two were running for their horses. Damn the luck. He'd have to fight them again, no doubt.

When he'd stopped in the village for supplies and to rest a bit, the last thing he'd expected to find had been the woman who was cousin to his sister-in-law Nora.

The last time he'd seen Catarina had been her brief visit to his castle after she and her family had saved his brother Ewan's life. She'd driven him near mad with her stubborn insults and he'd gladly bidden her farewell and had hoped to never lay eyes on her again.

Apparently his luck hadn't changed for the better in recent months.

Still, he owed this woman his brother's life and as such he was determined to save her from whatever mess she'd gotten herself into.

"Why are those men after you?" he asked over his shoulder.

"My father, Lucifer roast his toes, sicced them on me."

"Your father?"

"Aye. There's a man he wants me to marry. Be damned before I go quietly to that altar."

Lochlan smiled in spite of their danger. He couldn't agree more with the sentiment. "I feel for your situation, lass. Did he hire them to abduct you?"

"How did you know?"

"The fact there's no Viktor or Bavel watching over you." Her uncle and cousin were extremely protective of her. Wherever she went, they followed. The only way she could be here without them would have been for the men after them to have taken her.

"They kidnapped me from the inn where we were resting. I'm sure both of them are worried sick."

No doubt. Personally, he'd be grateful for the peace her absence would bring. But that was another matter.

He felt her turning behind him. "They're gaining on us."

Cursing, he looked to verify the truth of her statement. "They are persistent."

"Like worms after sunshine."

Lochlan was bemused by her expression, creative though it was. "Just how much did your father pay them for your abduction?"

"I don't think it's the payment that spurs them on so much as the fear of his wrath."

"And who is your father to warrant such terror?"

"Philip," she said simply.

Lochlan frowned. "Philip who?"

She duplicated his scowl. "Were you not listening when they told you? Philip Capet."

Lochlan froze as that name penetrated his mind. "*King* Philip of France?"

"Is there another?"

A sick feeling went through him. Lochlan had never felt more foolish in all his life, which, considering the fact he'd often run herd on four wayward brothers, said much for the moment. "Are you telling me that I have just abducted a princess of France from royal custody?"

"Nay, Lochlan MacAllister. You've just liberated a Moldavian princess from a man who thinks he can force her to marry against her will just because he says so."

He ground his teeth in anger. "I thought you were a peasant."

"That depends on whom you ask."

A feeling of dread clenched him. "If I don't receive a satisfactory answer from you, my lady, I'm going to slow down and ask the men who are following us exactly what *they* think."

Cat growled at his words. No wonder she hated this man. He was inflexible and stringent. She doubted if ever he'd met a rule he didn't absolutely love. "Fine then. My mother was the illegitimate daughter of a Moldavian prince and a peasant. Her father brought her to court when she was a young woman and there she met a man named Philip who shared her love of horses . . . they shared other things as well and she soon found herself pregnant with me. Since Philip wasn't free to marry her and she wanted no one else, she left her father's court to live with her mother's people. There I was raised until I was old enough for my father to see a political advantage to having a daughter tied to the Moldavian and Hungarian monarchies—even if I am illegitimate. And since that day of his sudden discovery, I have been on the move, trying my best to avoid any and all contact with him."

"Did you not think this information might prove pertinent to me before I threatened your guards?"

"Of course not. Besides, I threatened them first and assaulted them as well."

"Hmmm and shall that be your testimony on my behalf when your father demands my head?"

She scoffed at him. "You're not really afraid of my father, are you?"

"For myself, nay, I fear nothing. However, I'm not merely a man, Catarina. I am the MacAllister, just as your father is France. Whatever actions I take affect the lives of every person who looks to me for leadership. And I will not see my people punished because you are willful and stubborn."

"What do you mean by that?"

"Simple. I'm taking you to your father."

Chapter 2

Cat wasn't sure if she'd heard that correctly or not. "You're planning to do what?"

"Take you to your father."

She didn't know what irked her more, his intent or that arrogant look on his face as he said it. "Why would you do that?"

"To keep him from declaring war on my people for starters. Do not forget that King Philip's sister happens to be the wife to Alexander Canmore. Alexander is one of the few who could do a lot of damage to my people."

She couldn't believe this. "So you're just going

to cow to my father like everyone else? And to think I thought you were made of sterner stuff."

His features hardened. "This isn't a game, Catarina. I hold the responsibility for every person who claims MacAllister lands as home."

She snorted dismissively. "Your shoulders are mighty narrow to carry so much weight."

He looked as offended as she meant for him to be. "My shoulders aren't narrow."

She glanced down at them. "Matter of opinion that. But then perhaps 'tis the bow of your back from stooping to kiss the feet of men like my father that makes them appear so."

He reined his horse in sharply to glower at her. "Have you no sense to insult me so?"

"I have plenty of sense to insult you even more. I'm the daughter of the king. What are you going to do to stop me?"

His nostrils flared as those blue eyes snapped fire at her. "Your father should have bent you over his knee."

"Violence. How perfectly masculine of you to resort to such a thought."

Lochlan snarled at her like a feral lion before he laid spurs to the horse's flanks. The sudden motion almost caused her to slip from her seat.

She was forced to wrap her arms around his

waist to keep from falling even though the thought of touching him made her ill. "Are you trying to kill me?"

"Nay, my lady. I'm trying only to calm down *before* I succeed in killing you."

Unable to stand it and do nothing, she leaned forward to nip his shoulder.

Lochlan yelped at the unexpected pain. "Did you bite me?"

"Aye and I'm going to do worse than that if you don't release me instantly."

"Fine," he snapped, reining his horse again. As soon as it was stopped, he turned in the saddle to look at her. "There you are, my lady. You're free."

She was aghast at his actions. "What?"

He gestured toward the ground. "You wish to run? Have at it."

Surely he wasn't serious . . . "You would abandon me to the wilderness? Alone?"

"Oh I assure you, 'tis the bears and wolves I pity should they run into the likes of you."

Rage filled her as she wished for the millionth time that she'd been born a man. If she had, she'd beat Lochlan MacAllister to an inch of his life. "You are a louse."

He looked past her to the guards, who were almost upon them now. "Here are your new friends.

I'm sure they will be most happy to see you safely home."

She glared at him before she jumped to the ground. "You foul . . . foul thing!" she spat before she gathered her skirts and started running on foot.

Lochlan sat back in his saddle as he watched her run as quickly as she could. She was swift-footed for a maid and his abandoning her was exactly what she deserved for her insults. But his satisfaction ended when he saw the guards catch up to her. The largest man, who was the size of a bear, grabbed her roughly, wrenching her from the ground by one arm before he tossed her in front of him over the back of his horse. She screamed and cursed, kicking her legs and trying to bite the man, who moved his leg out of harm's reach and kept her in place with one hand.

Lochlan cringed at the sight of her riding on her stomach. He'd been forced to do it a time or two and knew firsthand how painful it could be.

What care you? 'Tis her father's business.

But the truth was he couldn't stand to see anyone, even a shrew such as she mistreated.

She bit you.

Again, true. Still, she'd saved Ewan's life . . . He owed her much for that.

Och now, Lochlan, don't even think it.

It was too late, he was already spurring his horse after them. The men took one look at him and immediately urged their horses faster.

"Wait!" Lochlan shouted. At the pace they were going, they would hurt her for sure.

But they didn't slow.

Unwilling to cause her more injury, he dropped back from the chase to trail them. Sooner or later they would be forced to stop and rest, then he could reclaim her from them and see her home without harm or abuse.

His shoulder twitched a reminder of her small bite. Well, *she* wouldn't be abused further. The verdict was still out on whether or not he'd be so fortunate.

As if he had time to see her home. He was on a quest to find more information about his brother Kieran, who'd vanished years ago. Since Kieran had left his sword and plaid on the shore of a loch, everyone had assumed he'd drowned himself after a woman had broken his heart. But no body had ever been found.

That story had never faltered until a duplicate plaid had shown up the night Lysander had been killed. Since that moment, Lochlan had been searching for clues about Kieran.

His quest had taken him to southern France, where he now believed his younger brother had gone after faking a suicide. A few days ago, Lochlan had been told of the knight who had last seen Kieran in the Holy Land. Stryder of Blackmoor.

Stryder was at tourney in Normandy, which was what had brought Lochlan here. That tourney would only last a few days more and it was imperative he reach it before the knights packed up and left.

If only he hadn't seen Catarina and her current plight. Whether he wanted to be or not, he was now involved. It wasn't in him to let her suffer even if she did deserve it.

Damn it to hell.

He'd been born with what his brother Braden called an ungodly sense of responsibility. His family had saddled him with it early and he'd never been able to shed it. Just once in his life he wished he could be more like Braden, Ewan, or Kieran who'd been able to live their lives for themselves. To care nothing of the consequences of their actions and how they affected others.

Instead, he was more than aware of how one person's thoughtlessness could impact those around him. Right now, he could ride off to attend his own business and Catarina could be maimed by the carelessness of her guards. By turning his back on her, anything could happen to her and it would be his fault for not helping her while he'd had the opportunity.

It was something that would weigh on his conscience for eternity.

"I'm not a martyr," he breathed angrily. But he was a man of his word and one of conviction . . . and she was a woman currently being abused by the very men hired to protect her.

That was wrong and he knew it.

So he followed them for almost an hour before they finally stopped to rest. Silently, he dismounted and left his horse to graze while he crept closer to where they'd stopped.

The guard holding Catarina practically threw her to the ground. "You run again and God as my witness, I'll break both your legs."

Catarina lifted her chin in defiance. "You wouldn't dare."

"Try it."

She stood with a grace and dignity that actually touched him. Lochlan had to give her credit, she was audacious as she confronted the larger man. She looked tiny and frail by comparison, but even so she wasn't intimidated. Her confidence astounded him.

Pieces of her long, black hair had come free of her braid and danced around her pale skin in the breeze, teasing at her cheeks and neck. Her dark eyes were livid and a slight blush darkened her cheeks. Truly, she was beautiful.

But only when she was silent.

The other man came forward to truss her up with a rope. She ducked his hands and shoved at him. Before she could move away, the man backhanded her so hard, she fell to the ground.

His temper snapping out of control, Lochlan crossed the distance between them in record time and grabbed the man as he moved to strike her again. He punched him hard, then slung him into the other, who'd come forward to help.

Cat couldn't believe her eyes as Lochlan turned, picked her up from the ground, and swung her onto the saddle of the horse closest to her. After handing her the reins, he slapped the horse's flanks, sending her on her way before he turned back to confront her guards.

Her cheek stung horribly from the blow the one man had given her. But she didn't pay any attention to it as she guided her horse away from the men. All she wanted was to be free of them forever. She kept her head bent low over the horse's neck as they flew down the road.

Her only thought escape, she didn't even bother to look behind her until she heard the sound of approaching hooves.

Afraid it was her guards again, Cat glanced back to see Lochlan there on his gray stallion. He didn't speak as he pulled alongside her, then grabbed her reins to slow her down.

"What are you doing?" she demanded.

He dodged her attempts to slap his hand away, then cupped her sore cheek. "I wanted to see what damage they'd wrought. Are you all right?"

His concern for her set her back. She wasn't used to such kindness from anyone other than Viktor or Bavel. "What do you care?"

Those steely eyes penetrated her with coldness. "Enough to have killed the man who did it. Now hold still and let me see the bruise."

Cat swallowed at his sharp tone. "You killed him?"

"Well I certainly didn't congratulate him on his strength. No doubt your father would have done far worse had he learned of it."

It was true. To strike royalty was a capital offense. But even so, she was surprised that Lochlan had taken such a personal interest in what had happened to her. It actually made her hatred of him lessen.

Lochlan dropped his hand to her wrist, the one that was crusted in blood. "What did they do to you?"

She pulled her hand away from him. "They tried to take me somewhere I didn't wish to go."

He shook his head at her. "Are you always so hell borne?"

"Nay, I can be quite pleasant when the mood strikes. But not when someone tries to impose his will on me with no regard to my feelings. Tell me, would you be so docile?"

"I'm a man."

She narrowed her eyes on him. "And your point?"

"I wasn't born to be subject to another man."

She laughed. "Aren't you? You've already told me how you're not free to do anything without it impacting your people. Do they not then own you?"

Lochlan arched a brow at her reasoning. She was frightfully quick. "That's not what I meant."

"Of course it wasn't. Being an ill-formed human, what would I know of rhetoric?"

More than she should. "I'm not Aristotle, my lady. I don't believe women are ill-formed men."

"Yet you accuse us of being hell borne."

"Nay," he said, leaning forward to stand his

ground. "I accused *you* of being hell borne, which you are. It was not meant as an indictment against all of your gender. Only an indictment against you."

Cat didn't know why, but something about his words amused her. And with the sunlight glinting in the reddish gold highlights of his hair, he was actually quite striking. There was an essence of power and nobility that bled from him. If she didn't know him for the irritant he was, he'd be quite pleasing to look upon.

Her horse stepped away from his, jarring her slightly. An urge to run from him went through her, but she'd seen enough of his horsemanship to know he could outrun her. If she wished to escape him, she'd have to be even more cunning than she'd been with the guards.

But first, she'd try logic. "I have no wish to return to my father. Will you help me to find Viktor and Bavel . . . please?"

She could see the uncertainty in his eyes.

She only prayed she could use that uncertainty to move him to her side. It would be much easier to find her family if she had someone with her. A lone woman traveling through the countryside invited much undue speculation and attention.

Not to mention danger. There were numerous

thieves and outlaws hiding in the forests who would love nothing more than to lay hands to an unguarded noblewoman.

"The guards are dead," she said softly. "No one will know you helped me. I can assure you that I will certainly tell no one. Please, Lochlan. All I want in life is to answer to no man. Surely you can understand that. My father would saddle me with a crown and a husband that I don't want. If you have any compassion inside you, then I beg you to be merciful. I would sooner you run me through with your sword than hand me over to them."

Lochlan didn't speak as he debated with himself. He knew the yoke she feared. There were times when it was oppressive and harsh and it weighed like an iron door on him. There wasn't a day in his life when he hadn't felt it choking him at some point.

Catarina was like a feral beast that would sooner gnaw its own limb off than be caught in a trap. A prince or king would demand complete obedience from her and if she failed to give it, her husband could, and most likely would, imprison her just as the English king had done his queen. For that matter, her husband could demand her life.

At the very least, she'd be beaten into submission. It was something he'd wish on no person. Not even her.

"Very well, Catarina. I will help you find your uncle and cousin, but first I must needs travel to Normandy to see a man about my brother."

She looked at him suspiciously. "Swear you this isn't a trick?"

"No trickery. I swear it on the souls of my brothers. I will stand by you and see you to Viktor and Bavel. What happens after I deliver you to them is your business."

Her eyes dazzled him with her spirit and happiness. "For that I would kiss you . . . if you weren't a cad."

In spite of the insult, her words amused him. "You do remember what happened the last time you insulted me, do you not?"

"Aye, but you did come back for me, didn't you?"

"Mayhap next time I won't."

"Perhaps . . ." She kicked her horse on ahead of him.

Beguiled by her spirit, Lochlan watched the way she rode. Her spine was straight and she moved in perfect synchronization with her horse. Her regal bearing was hard to miss and yet he'd been stupid enough to not catch on to it the first time they'd met. Of course, he'd been a bit preoccupied with Ewan and the mess his brother had gotten himself into with Canmore when Ewan had run off with the man's daughter . . .

Still, Lochlan should have seen it.

Now there was no mistaking her birthright and yet there was also a feral quality about her. This was a woman who loved life and she didn't try to hide that fact. While other noblewomen conducted themselves with the utmost care for what others thought of them, she lived with abandon. If she was happy, she laughed. If she was angry . . .

She bit.

God help whatever fool ever gave his heart to such a woman. He'd never have peace in his home. She would ever argue and fight until her husband either gave up or gave in.

Shaking his head, he caught up to her and forced her to slow a bit. "We need to spare the horses as much as possible."

"Should we walk then?"

He was taken aback by her suggestion. "Are you willing?"

"Should I not be?"

Most women of his acquaintance weren't. While beautiful, the countryside was a bit jagged. It was tiring to walk for very long. "Nay." He reined his horse and slid to the ground. Before he could make his way over to assist her, she was on the ground herself, stroking the horse's forehead as it nuzzled her shoulder.

She cast a smile in his direction before she began making her way down the road on foot. He was mystified and captivated by her sudden turn of temperament.

"You are of a merry mood."

She threw her arms out and leaned back as she walked. "I'm free—at least for another day. That alone is cause for celebration." She straightened to look at him. "Do you never celebrate the fact that you're here, right now, alive and well with the sun on your face and the birds singing around you? That the sky above is a particularly striking shade of blue?"

He was beginning to wonder if the woman wasn't possessed of moon-poisoning. "Nay. I have to say that I've never considered such."

She frowned at him. "Do you not dance when you hear music?"

"I'm laird of my clan, lass. 'Tis unseemly for me to do such. Besides, whatever woman I choose to partner with immediately assumes more to my intention than a mere dance."

Cat paused as she heard his emotionless words. Poor man to fear something so simple as a dance.

"I can't imagine a life without dance. 'Twould be like living without laughter." She cocked her head to look at him as she remembered her brief stay with him in Scotland. "You don't laugh either, do you?"

"When the occasion calls for it."

"Rarely you mean."

He let out a long breath as if exasperated by her and their conversation. "If you are wishing to list my shortcomings, you needn't bother. I assure you, I'm quite aware of each and every one of them."

Cat heard the pain behind his tone and decided to give him a reprieve. It was obvious that someone in his past had spent a great deal of time telling him what his shortcomings were.

"I wasn't listing your shortcomings, Lochlan. My intent was only to make conversation with you to pass the time. If you'd rather we walk in silence, then I shall try to manage it."

He inclined his head to her in a manner that was so noble it was all she could do not to chide him for that as well. "Forgive me for my assumption, my lady. Please, by all means, continue on with your interrogation."

Cat cocked a brow at his unexpected retort. "Was that a jest?"

"A poor one apparently if you must ask."

She laughed. "But it was an attempt and for that I'm proud of you." She watched him for a moment as he walked slightly ahead of her. He held a powerful, manly gait. It was cocksure and straight—as if he expected to have to defend himself at any moment. It was a warrior's gait, not noble. His gaze continually searched the area around them as if looking for threat.

There was something unbelievably compelling about that. And she found it strange that he was here without a servant or guard.

"Have you been alone on your entire journey?"

He glanced back at her. "For the most part. Aye. Pagan left my company before I boarded the boat to leave England."

She smiled at the reminder of her old friend. Pagan had left the company of her and her family while they were in Scotland to look after personal matters. He'd been a churlish man, but still she'd valued his friendship. "Oh how I miss him. He was always so caustic and morbid."

"And you miss that?"

"Aye. He could be quite amusing with his rancor."

Instead of responding, Lochlan drew up short and motioned for her to stop and remain quiet.

Cat would have asked him what was wrong, but by his actions, she could tell that silence was the better part of valor.

He peered into the trees around them and tilted his head as if listening for something.

She moved to stand just beside him. "Is something amiss?" she whispered beneath her breath.

"I'm not sure."

She swallowed at his barely audible words. And as he continued to search the area with his gaze, she became acutely aware of just how close she stood to him. She'd forgotten how large a man Lochlan really was. When surrounded by his brothers, he tended to get lost in the mix.

But like this . . . he was extremely unsettling. His shoulders were broad and very well muscled. The ties of his tunic had come loose, showing her the corded muscles of his chest while his hand rested on the hilt of his sword, as if ready to battle.

Personally, she'd always thought of blond men as a bit plain and feminine. Yet there was nothing plain or womanish about him. He had sharp, chiseled features and his eyes were searing with their beauty and intelligence.

But what surprised her most was the sudden urge she had to reach out and touch his cheek to feel the stubble that graced it. She didn't even know why she wanted to touch it, and yet that compulsion was so strong that she wasn't sure how she kept from complying.

Lochlan glanced down, then froze as he caught the hot look on Catarina's face. He was used to seeing lust in a woman's eyes, but not in hers. It was both disturbing and arousing. Given the less-than-friendly nature of most of their encounters, he couldn't believe that such a look from her actually made his body heat up. A suicidal part of him even wanted to kiss her.

Och, man, stand down. You don't want to be tasting the lips of a viper. She's a hellion for sure and the last thing you need is to be mixing with a woman who's going to complicate your already complicated life.

It was true. He only wanted peace. There was enough turmoil in dealing with his people, brothers, and mother. The last thing he wanted was to invite more misery and argument into his home. He wanted a lass who was pliant and calm-natured. One who would soothe him, not rile his spirit more.

Clearing his throat, he stepped back from her and retook his horse's reins. "Whatever I felt seems to be naught. Let's keep moving." He started back down the road.

She moved to walk beside him. "So how are

your brothers? Is Ewan taking care of my cousin or has Nora skinned him yet?"

He kept his gaze forward and not on the fetching sight she made standing beside him. "They're all well. And while Nora has threatened to skin him a bit, Ewan looks completely content to let her."

"But you're worried."

Those words succeeded in making him look at her. "What makes you say that?"

"My mother held second sight and I have a bit of it myself. You're not at peace where your family's concerned, I can feel it."

It was true. There was much unrest at home. Braden had told their mother of Kieran's plaid and now his mother wept with fear over the son who was lost to the world. Lochlan had promised her, he wouldn't return until he knew for certain what had happened to Kieran.

"At least I'm not running from them," he reminded her of her own family plight.

"True. My father is a stubborn man. Like you. But I'm surprised that you've come alone. Who is leading your clan while you're away?"

"Braden and Ewan are seeing to it, along with my mother's help."

"That seems so out of character for you. I can't imagine you entrusting anyone with your clan."

He chose to ignore the biting sarcasm of her tone. "I'm not entrusting just anyone, lass. It's my brothers and they are well versed in clan politics. Besides, I couldn't ask my brothers to leave their wives and children for this long and I wouldn't trust such a journey to anyone but family. I was the only one who could do it. So here I am."

"And have you found word of Kieran?"

"Aye. He left Scotland and went to the Holy Land in search of our brother Sin."

"But he never found him."

He shook his head. "There were many who knew Kieran though. The last anyone saw, he was with a knight named Stryder of Blackmoor. I was told that Lord Stryder would know what became of Kieran."

"And if you find this brother—"

"I shall beat him until he bleeds and begs me for mercy," Lochlan growled.

"Why so angry?"

He didn't answer. Instead, he remembered the last time he'd seen his brother.

Kieran had been drunk, sitting in their childhood nursery as he wallowed about in pain. "Do you remember the day Isobail first came here?"

Lochlan had been trying to take the mead from him, but he'd refused to let it go. Portions of it had splashed Kieran's tunic, molding it to his chest. "I remember."

Kieran had curled himself protectively around the jug. His eyes bloodshot, he'd stared up at Lochlan. "How did you know she was evil?"

Knowing his brother needed compassion more than thrashing, Lochlan had stepped back to answer the question. "She was calculating. Her gaze was only warm when you were looking at her. The moment you looked away, there was a coldness that would settle about her." And they had fought that night of her arrival when Lochlan had told his brother what he'd seen. Kieran had called him a jealous bastard because he had the love of Isobail while Lochlan had nothing.

Kieran had sniffed back his drunken tears. "I should have listened to you. But what do you know of love or women? I've never even seen you with one. I've oft wondered if you're even interested in them."

Lochlan had frozen at the bitter accusation in Kieran's voice. "What say you?"

Kieran's gaze had pierced him. "You know what I'm saying. I think it's men who hold your interest. Is that why you turned Isobail from me? You were jealous that one of us had a woman while you can't even approach one."

Rage had suffused him, but Lochlan had refused to give in to it. "You're drunk."

"I'm not the only one who thinks it. Braden, Ewan . . . even our mother and father. Da told me of the whore he'd bought for you that you spurned. He said you were nothing but a worthless gelding."

Lochlan had backhanded his brother for that. Aye, he'd turned the woman away and paid her because no human being should have to sell themselves for food. It'd angered him that his father would be so callous. That he thought no more of people than what he could use them for.

Nor did Lochlan want to be as his father, a philanderer who held no regard for the women or bastards he left behind. He'd seen the results of trifling with others' emotions. It'd ruined his mother and brother Sin, and countless others. The last thing Lochlan had ever wanted was to know a child of his was hurting.

Kieran had come at him then with a sword and they'd fought. In the end, Lochlan had disarmed his brother and sent him slamming to the ground.

Kieran had lain on the floor, flat on his back, glaring up at him. "For once in your life, Lochlan, be a man. Kill me."

Lochlan had sheathed his sword. "I am a man, Kieran. Believe me. There's a lot more to manhood than fathering bastards and stealing women from others. I'm not the one crying in my cups over the fact my brother ran off with my woman. If you'd been half the man you think you are, then you'd have been able to hold on to her." It'd been a lie. Isobail's heart had been frigid and she'd only been using all of them, but at the time, he'd wanted to hurt Kieran as much as his brother had hurt him.

Kieran had laughed. "At least I've had a woman in my bed. I'm not the weak-kneed Ganymede, hiding in my father's shadow."

Lochlan had tightened his grip on the hilt of his sword. Afraid he might yet kill his own brother, he'd turned to leave.

"That's right, you coward. Run from the drunken unarmed sot on the floor. You're afraid of everything—women, conflict, and life. You might as well be dead for all the living you've done. You're useless, Lochlan. Useless!"

He'd turned to glare at his brother. "At least I'm not trying to spread misery with my life. Want to talk about useless? All you've ever been able to do is make everyone who loves you weep in grief. You're the one who should be dead."

Those had been the last words he'd spoken to

his brother and they had burned a hole in his heart every day since they'd found Kieran's sword and plaid and had assumed him dead.

No one knew of that moment in the nursery. No one knew how much guilt Lochlan felt and how much hurt. It was his alone to bear.

And if Kieran was alive and had put him through this for no other reason than selfish vanity, he would kill him for sure this time.

But none of that would take away the sting of truth. Because of his father's reckless infidelities and the responsibility for running the clan while his father was drunk, Lochlan had become isolated very early in his life. He'd done his best to keep the truth of his father's character from everyone. His mother, his brothers, and his clan.

The only time he'd ever sought the comfort of a woman, she'd betrayed him foully and it was that betrayal he could never get past. There was no way he would ever open himself up to another person for that kind of pain again. He'd had enough of it.

Catarina cleared her throat, dragging his attention back to her. "I asked you a question, Lochlan, and it seems to have gotten you lost in thought. Are you all right?"

"I am fine, my lady."

"Hmmm . . . my mother used to say that men will only admit to being fine when they're hiding something. What are you hiding?"

He let out a long, tired breath. "You are relentless with your questions."

"And you are very much like your brother Ewan. That's not an insult, by the way. I happen to like Ewan a great deal . . . when he's not being stubborn. But he was never one to talk much either. He said it was because he could never get a word in while his brothers were talking. I can only assume he meant Braden and Sin since neither you nor Ewan speaks."

Lochlan grew quiet as he realized he was being charmed by her. If he were Braden, he'd probably have her naked beneath him within the next quarter hour. But those kinds of flirtations never appealed to him . . . actually that wasn't true. The thought of them appealed to him greatly. There was nothing he'd like more than to silence her speech with a kiss and take her to the copse of trees ahead for a quick tryst.

It was the consequences of what happened after the sex that kept him from acting out his fantasies. There would be the fear of an unplanned baby and she would expect more from him than just a kiss and a tumble. He'd spent too many days drying the tears of women who were upset at his brothers to want to deal that pain to another. Not to mention all the years of his mother's weeping over his father's heartless dalliances. He liked to think he was a better man than to let his animal instincts override his humanity.

Lochlan paused as he caught sight of something out of the corner of his eye. He had the worst feeling they were being followed.

But it wasn't possible. The guards were both dead and no one else knew where he was.

Catarina eyed him suspiciously. "If you keep that up, you're going to make me nervous."

"Forgive me."

Cat didn't know what to think of her escort. He was so proper and rigid, which was what irritated her about him. He reminded her too much of her father. Always concerned about appearances, her father had refused even to hold her hand when she'd been a child. Royalty was expected to hide everything. They lived restrained and that wasn't her. She had too much of her mother in her for that.

It was why she was running from what her father wanted even though it wasn't in her to run at all. She'd always been the kind of person to stand her ground, but in this she had no voice. Her father would preach to her of obligation and duty. He would somehow guilt her into a relationship that was doomed and life was too short to be spent in a miserable trap with a man who expected her to laugh never. A man who would dictate what she wore, how she conducted herself, and if she could even be seen in public.

Cat wanted laughter and dance. Happiness. Most of all, she wanted to love. She never wanted to reach out to a man again in her life and have him flinch or step away. She wanted someone who could touch her without caring what others would think.

She would never forget that day as a young woman when she'd been in a village with her uncle Bavel. They'd gone to town for supplies and while there she'd seen a soldier returning from battle. He'd been on foot, ragged and unkempt.

Even so, a shrill scream of delight had split the air a moment before a woman only a few years older than her had dropped her basket and run to him. He'd scooped her up in his arms and had twirled around with her, laughing and kissing her.

That was what Cat wanted. An unrestrained love. Passion. To know that her lover held no regard for anyone but her. It was as unrealistic as flying pigs, but she'd seen it once and that moment had given her hope. It was a hope she clung to tenaciously.

She refused to settle for anything less.

"So tell me something, Lochlan?" she asked, trying to break the awkward silence between them. "Have you married your bride yet?"

He appeared startled by her question. "Pardon?"

"Ewan told me that you were negotiating a marriage contract with another clan. I was wondering if you'd married her yet?"

A coldness came over his features. "Her father wishes it."

"But not you?"

"It would make sense to align our clans. Hers has a great deal of farmland and they are known fighters. It would increase our numbers and shore up our defenses in the south."

She tsked at him. "Oh, Lochlan . . . I pity your bride. Is that what you'll tell her on your wedding night? My people thank you for the marriage, my lady. Our union will give us more farmland?"

He paused to frown at her. "You cannot live your life with wild abandon forever, Catarina. Sooner or later you have to grow up and realize there are consequences for freedom."

"Aye, laughter. Fun. Grave consequences indeed."

He shook his head. "You're just like Braden. And in his ever quest for freedom lay a hundred broken hearts who will never get over his carefree abandon. Do you not care who you hurt?"

"Of course I care. I've never hurt anyone intentionally."

"What about the bite you took out of my shoulder?"

She lifted her chin boldly. "You were suppressing me and I was defending myself. My laughter and dance have never hurt anyone."

His blue eyes were chilling. "You think not? Have you any idea how many men might have seen you dance and believe that you're attracted to them? When you rebuff them, it hurts, whether you mean for it to or not."

She scowled at the anger in his tone. "My God, how many times have you been hurt to feel that way?"

"Never. I don't allow myself the luxury of those emotions, but I've dried enough tears from women who lament and mourn the careless behavior of people who play with their emotions. 'Tis cruel to trifle with others."

Well, she wouldn't have to worry about him try-

ing to seduce her, not that she'd ever be suscep-
tible to him. He was unbearable.

Cat fell silent as they walked. There really
wasn't much to say to someone who was so different from her. It was obvious he was content
to live a restrained life and she was most certain
their views on every topic would be as diametri-
cally opposed. Unlike her, Lochlan didn't seem to
thrive on debate. Rather he preferred peaceful silence and the last thing she wanted to do was agi-
tate the best hope she had of avoiding her father's
plans.

After an hour, Lochlan helped her mount her
horse and they rode quietly until they reached
another small settlement. It was late evening and
there was quite a bit of activity as people rushed
to finish their business before nightfall.

Lochlan slid to the ground in front of the village
stable, then turned to help her down. Several of
the townsmen turned to study them. It was obvious they didn't get many strangers here.

An older man came out of the barn, scratching
the back of his neck. Around the age of threescore,
he had fluffy gray hair and thick brows.

Lochlan handed him the reins of his horse.
"Could you please give them extra oats?"

The man frowned at Lochlan. "What's that?"

Lochlan held out his coin. "Could you please give the horses extra oats."

The man twisted up his face in distaste. "What you speaking, English?"

Lochlan couldn't have looked any more offended had he tried.

Cat realized the man couldn't understand Lochlan's Norman French through his thick brogue. She stepped forward to smooth the matter between them. "We need to stable the horses for the night, good sir. He wishes you to give them extra oats."

"Then why didn't he say that?"

Lochlan's scowl deepened as the man took his money and left with the horses. "'Tis what I said."

Cat had to force herself not to laugh at his ire. She was certain Lochlan wouldn't appreciate it in the least. "Aye, but you have quite an accent there and I'm sure he's not heard it often."

The man returned to them and cleared his throat before he spoke to Cat. "By the way, my lady, you might want to tell folks he's mute and speak for him. We don't like foreigners here, especially the English."

Lochlan's nostrils flared. "I'm not English," he said between clenched teeth.

Cat feigned a seriousness she didn't feel. "In his world there's no difference between you and them."

"There's a lot of difference."

"I know that, but to a French peasant, you're just another stranger and English or Scottish makes no difference."

A tic worked in his jaw.

Cat patted him on the arm. "Come, my lord, and I'll see about getting us a place to eat and rest."

"You're enjoying this, aren't you?"

"More than you'll ever know."

Lochlan watched as she flounced on ahead of him, gloating in her smugness. Truth be told, he'd had quite a few problems with people not understanding his French even though he was fluent in it. It angered him that he was now forced to rely on a woman who could barely tolerate him.

As they neared what appeared to be a small hostel, he heard a boy pleading in the tanner's shop.

"Please, sir, my father will be ruthlessly angry. He told me that he needed proper payment this time."

"And I've given you your payment, boy. Now get out before I thrash you."

"But sir—"

The boy's voice was cut off by the sound of a slap. An instant later, a child no older than ten stumbled out, holding his cheek. Lanky and small, his brown eyes were bright with tears.

Lochlan pulled the boy to a stop as he started past. "Are you all right?"

He recoiled. "Please, my lord. I have nothing for you to take."

Lochlan shook his head. "I don't want to take from you, lad. I just want to know if you were dealt with fairly or not?"

Cat paused as she realized Lochlan wasn't behind her. She hastened back to find him with a boy, outside a small shop.

The boy's cheek was bright crimson and bore the outline of a large hand. That sight alone was enough to infuriate her.

His voice trembled as he spoke to Lochlan. "I brought the hides as my father bade me, but the tanner only paid half his usual fee."

Before she could blink, Lochlan took the boy inside the store to confront the owner. She followed after them, but Lochlan didn't seem to know she was even there as he faced the tanner.

The man's eyes widened as he took in the size of Lochlan and the presence of his sheathed sword.

"The child says you be owing him payment."

The tanner's gaze narrowed angrily. "What lies you telling, boy?"

"None, sir, please. My father will beat me if I bring home less than what he expects."

The tanner curled his lip as he threw a stack of hides at the boy. "You're lucky I paid you anything at all. These are worthless to me. Your drunken father ruined most of them. Now get out of my sight before I have you arrested for theft."

The boy tucked his chin to his chest and turned, but Lochlan stopped him. He knelt before the child. "Let me see your coins."

Tears welled in the boy's eyes as he opened his hand to show a single copper coin.

"And how much more are you supposed to have?"

"A franc, my lord."

Lochlan loosened the strings of his purse, then handed the child two francs.

The boy looked at him in disbelief. "Thank you, my lord. May God bless you."

Lochlan inclined his head before the child ran out of the store. Then he stood and turned a terrifying glower toward the tanner, who took two steps back. He threw several coins at the man. "That's for your charity, but you need to better counsel your hand. Remember, a dog will only take so many kicks before it turns vicious. The boy you abuse today could well become the man who will return the favor to you when he's grown."

Cat stepped back as Lochlan stalked past her.

She met the tanner's eyes and saw the fear he held. It was doubtful he'd ever strike another child. Grateful for that, she rushed after Lochlan.

"That was very kind of you."

"Don't patronize me, Catarina."

She pulled him to a stop. "I never patronize anyone. What you did was extremely kind. I'm sure you have no idea what that single act meant to that child."

"Believe me, I do know."

There was something about the conviction in his voice that made her want to hug him. If she didn't know better, she'd think that he knew exactly how that abused child felt. But she'd seen the love his family had for him. They were so close that there was no way he could comprehend the misery that child most likely knew.

Still, he reminded her much of a wounded lion and she didn't understand why. He was so stern and rigid . . . so powerful that the thought of him being wounded by anything was incongruous. Even though Ewan was physically a much larger man than Lochlan, he lacked the lethal quality that seemed ingrained in the MacAllister.

And Lochlan was even more rigid now than he'd been earlier.

Sighing with the thought, she led him toward

the hostel. As soon as they entered, several of the workers turned a suspicious eye to them. Cat made her way to the man in an apron who was directing one of the maids.

"Pardon, sir? We have need of a room for the night."

His gaze narrowed heatedly on Lochlan. "You always let your woman speak for you?"

Lochlan's nostrils flared before he took a step toward the man, who immediately squeaked and put a great distance between them.

Cat put her hand on his chest to stop Lochlan's advance.

The man gulped before he nodded toward the stairs. "There's one room at the top, third door on your right."

She smiled warmly. "Thank you. We'll also be needing food."

"It'll be ready shortly."

She inclined her head to him before she took Lochlan's hand to lead him toward the stairs.

Lochlan's anger melted as he felt her soft hand clutching his. Only his sisters-in-law and mother had ever done such a thing. It was a familiar touch and yet this one rocked him to the core of his being. It ignited his blood and made him acutely aware of the fact she was taking him to a room with a bed . . .

His cock hardened at the thought.

She led him into the room, then closed the door behind her.

The heat in his groin was unbearable as his gaze fell to a bed that was far too tiny. "We should have gotten two rooms. This is highly improper."

"Perhaps, but what do you think they'd make of a man and woman traveling together alone? 'Tis safer if they believe us married."

She had a point, but it did nothing to alleviate the fiery pain in his groin. It was fierce and hard, and made him wish he'd never gotten involved with her.

He dropped his saddlebags by the window. "I'll sleep on the floor."

Cat was amused by his words until she heard the sound of a large group of horses outside. It sounded much like a small army had ridden into town. Moving to the window, she pushed open the shutters to see a group of soldiers. She pulled back with a gasp.

"What?" Lochlan asked as he joined her to see them below.

"They're my father's men."

Chapter 3

Lochlan listened quietly as he watched the men dismount below. He didn't think much of it until the captain stopped a man on the street.

"We're seeking a young woman." He held his hand out to the height of his shoulder. "She's about this tall with black hair and dark eyes and would be traveling alone. She answers to the name Catarina."

Luckily the man shook his head as Lochlan did his best to try and remember if he'd called her by name around any of the villagers.

"At least they think I'm still alone," she whispered to him.

That was something, but they were a long way from being out of the woods on this one. "Have you ever seen any of them before?"

She looked down, then shook her head. "I think not, but 'tis hard to say for certain. There are a lot of people at my father's court and it's hard to see their faces clearly from up here."

He cursed. They could try to slip out the back and escape, but like as not that would make the soldiers suspicious. If he were smart, he'd abandon her to them. But that would be unchivalrous and he'd given her his word.

"The best course of action is to stay here, I think, and let them search the town, then leave."

Catarina looked about sheepishly. "You think they'll search the rooms here?"

"'Tis possible."

She let out a frustrated breath. "I should go to them then before they find me."

"Excuse me?"

"It would be prudent. If they find me with you, there's no telling what they might do to you. I'm sure I can escape them again."

He cast a doubtful look at the large number of men searching the town. Granted, she was a hellion, but their number was such that even he would have a hard time escaping them. "I promised I'd see you to your uncle, Catarina, and so I shall."

"Aye, but what of your people?"

"The guards below know nothing of me or my people. So long as you don't tell them who I am, my people will be safe."

"You would do that for me?"

"I'm a man of my word. Always. I promised I'd take you to Bavel and so I shall."

Cat smiled up at him. "I was wrong about you, Lochlan MacAllister. You're not as obnoxious as I thought. You're actually quite heroic." And as she spoke, she realized exactly how handsome he was. Even though his hair was tousled and he wasn't freshly shaven, he was extremely compelling. She couldn't imagine any man being more attractive.

And as she looked at him, his eyes darkened as he stared at her lips with an unfathomable hunger. That gaze was so hot that she could almost feel his lips on hers. Feel his body pressing against her. She shivered, wanting to know what his kiss would feel like.

Lochlan had just dipped his head toward hers when a sharp knock caused both of them to jump.

"By the order of the king, open this door!"

Lochlan motioned her to silence before he went

to open it. Cat swallowed in fear of what was going to happen.

With dark hair and a stern face, the guard took a step into the room. His gaze narrowed on Cat before he took in the size and bearing of Lochlan. His anger slipped down a notch. "Forgive me, my lord, but I was told you called the woman with you Catarina?"

"By whom?"

"A woman on the street. She said you were both foreigners."

Still Lochlan bore the arrogant stance of a man greatly perturbed by the guard's interruption. "What of it?"

"I'm looking for the king's daughter, Catarina. It is imperative that we find and return her." He cast a meaningful gaze to Cat who let her face melt to the most charming expression she could muster.

"Och now, sir," Cat said, mimicking Lochlan's Scottish brogue. "Surely you don't be thinking me a French princess now, do you?" She took a step forward and wrapped her arm around Lochlan's. "I'm flattered to be sure, but unfortunately there's only me and my husband here."

The guard frowned. "But your name is Catarina?"

"Catriona. Similar I suppose to French ears, but not the same."

He nodded as relief cut across his brow. "I understand completely. Please forgive my interruption."

Cat didn't breathe until the man had shut the door and she heard his footsteps recede down the hallway.

Lochlan was still scowling at her. "Wherever did you get that accent?"

She wrinkled her nose at him. "Listening to you and your brothers. I tend to pick them up quite easily."

"You can say that. It sounded there for a moment as if you were born to it and Catriona . . . brilliant."

She curtsied to him. "I try."

She saw the fire return to his eyes before he excused himself and left her alone in the room to rest. He exited so quickly that she didn't even have time to speak.

His actions would have amused her a lot more had she not felt the same heat around him. There was something about him so unsettling and desirable that it was all she could do not to force him to kiss her.

Don't forget you hate him. He is everything you loathe in a man.

He was also kind to an unknown peasant boy and protective of her. Everyone had faults. He just had more than his share. But that being said, his positive factors went a long way in smoothing over those faults.

Pushing that thought away, she went to his saddlebags to see if he had anything she might nibble on until their food was ready. She'd escaped her guards earlier and hadn't had a chance to eat a single bite all day. Truthfully, she was famished.

As she reached the windows, her attention was drawn again to the soldiers outside. And as she spied a man she knew, her heart stopped beating.

Myles D'Anjou . . .

She ran back to the bed, away from the window. Closing her eyes, she whispered a small prayer that he would leave before he caught sight of her. Why was he even here? Why would a nobleman travel with common guards trying to find her?

To win points with her father, of course. Myles's family had angered her father by siding with King Henry over some matter and since then her father had been suspicious of them.

She wanted to curse her luck. Myles had been the first of her father's courtiers to make his intention to court her known. Luckily, her father had rejected his offers. He didn't trust the man and neither did she. Myles would gladly hand her over without a moment's hesitation.

Or worse, he would do something to try and force her father to make her marry him.

How she wished she could tell Lochlan of his presence. But if she knew her Highland lord, he wouldn't speak to the man anyway.

You're worrying for naught.

She hoped that was true. God help her if Myles met Lochlan and learned of her presence here.

"Excuse me?"

Lochlan paused as he left the shop and saw a man about a head shorter approaching him. "Can I help you?"

He was a nobleman unless Lochlan missed his guess, but not a wealthy one. Though his boots were a finer grade of leather, they were old and worn. His dark blue tunic and hose also denoted nobility, however, they had a simple trim, not the ornate ones preferred by those with coin. Even his sword was old and in need of repair. "I'm looking for a woman."

Lochlan snorted. "Well then you're out of luck with me, lad. Last I checked, I'm definitely not female."

The man gave him a less-than-amused stare. "I heard you came to town with a woman who sounds a lot like the one I've been looking for."

"I've already had word with another of your men. She's not the one you seek."

"Really? And I'm just to take your word on that matter?"

"Most people do."

His gaze dropped to Lochlan's sword, which was encrusted with rubies and emeralds around the hilt. "Are you noble?"

"Aye, with blood ties to three thrones."

That gave the man pause. "Where are you from, my lord?"

"I think I've answered enough of your questions. My wife waits for me and I've no wish to keep her waiting. I'm sure as a man in search of a woman, you can understand my urgency to get back to her."

Lochlan stepped past him. From the corner of his eye, he saw the man call another guard to him. Damn. This didn't bode well. Grinding his teeth, he swept his gaze to the others who were questioning people and searching places where Catarina might be hiding. He'd fought such odds before, but he'd at least had another sword in hand when he'd done so and he hadn't been dragging a woman along with him. A fight with the king's guard could be bloody indeed.

Trying to put that thought out of his mind, he entered the hostel, where a maid was slicing roasted venison. He paused beside her and handed her coin. "Could you bring two platters and wine to our room?"

Her eyes widened as she saw the amount he'd given her. "Aye, my lord. I'll be there posthaste."

He inclined his head to her before he headed up the stairs and into the room where Catarina was waiting in a corner with the window drawn tightly closed.

He'd never seen her so quelled. "Is something amiss?"

"Aye," she said in a low tone. "I do know one of the men below."

"Let me guess. A short, beady-eyed fellow who wreaks of garlic and sweat?"

"Myles D'Anjou. I take it you met the swine."

He nodded. "He cornered me on the street."

"What did you tell him?" she asked in a fearful tone.

"Absolutely nothing. Think you he'll listen?"

"Doubtful. He's possessed of a terrible nosiness. So much so that Viktor threatened to cut the joint off and hand it to him if it would give us peace from him putting it where it doesn't belong."

Cat pushed herself up from the floor as Lochlan approached her with a wrapped bundle.

He held it out to her.

"What is this?"

"Something I thought you might like."

Frowning, she untied the ribbon and pulled back the serge to find a soft linen chemise, a dark blue kirtle, and another of bright green. The gowns were absolutely lovely.

Lochlan put a few feet of distance between them before he spoke. "The tailor said that the gowns lace tight enough to fit most maids."

Cat was speechless as she ran her hand over the finely woven cloth. The last thing she'd expected had been so costly a gift. Indeed, they must have been intended for a lady and Lochlan would have been forced to bribe the tailor quite a bit to let loose such finery. "Why did you purchase this?"

Still he refused to look at her. "You have no clothing, my lady, and I know how women value such things. I didn't want you to feel awkward when we reached the tourney."

She swallowed at his unexpected kindness. It was truly thoughtful. Her heart pounding, she moved to stand before him. "Thank you, Lochlan," she said before she placed a chaste kiss to his cheek.

Lochlan couldn't breathe as he felt the softness of her lips on his skin. Unable to stand it, he turned his head and took possession of her mouth. He growled at the sweet taste of her.

Cat dropped her bundle to the floor so that she could cup Lochlan's face in her hands. Oh the taste of this man. He was tender and feral. Everything about him made her burn. She'd never been kissed like this. She felt both devoured and cherished. It didn't make sense that she could be so attracted to him.

Suddenly a knock sounded.

Lochlan pulled back with a fierce growl. Cat could do nothing more than stand there as he went to the door and threw it open. The maid in the hallway actually squeaked in terror of his stern countenance.

"Your food, my lord."

Raking a hand through his hair, Lochlan stood back to let her enter. He cast Cat a look that singed her to the spot.

As quickly as she could, the maid left their food on the small table by the window and beat a hasty retreat.

Lochlan would have been amused by the woman's actions had his groin not been on fire. As it was, all he could think of was either pouring water in his lap or making use of the bed behind him. Unfortunately, neither was a feasible option.

Catarina leaned over the food and sighed. He'd seldom seen a more blissful look as she tore a bit of bread and placed it in her mouth.

"Hungry?"

"Famished," she breathed. Then she gave him a most impish stare. "Should you ever find yourself on the run, I recommend eating before you bash your guard over the head and slip away. 'Tis rather hard to stop and eat while fleeing. They tend to catch up to you then."

He smiled at that. "I shall keep that in mind should I ever awaken in chains."

Lochlan joined her at the table as she poured wine for both of them.

She swallowed a bit of wine before she spoke again. "Of course, we did stop for the night . . ."

"And they appear to have caught up to us."

She nodded. "Think you we should flee as soon as they quiet down?"

Lochlan glanced out the window, where it was already growing dark. "Let's see what they do first. With any luck, they'll clear out. Besides, we will need to rest. Better here than on horseback while trying to flee. Not to mention the horses are exhausted and need to rest even more than we do."

"Aye, but I truly hate to wait."

"And I believe that impatience was what had you caught in your earlier predicament, was it not?"

She wrinkled her nose at him. There was something so charming about that look that he couldn't even fathom it. They finished their meal in silence while Lochlan considered the best course of action.

Moving to the window, he kept waiting for the orders for the soldiers to leave, but they seemed entrenched. His only hope was that they didn't intend to stay the night. The stress of this continued waiting was also starting to wear on Catarina.

"Would you mind giving me a moment? I'd like to wash and change clothes."

Lochlan nodded. "There's a brush in my bags if you have wish of it."

"Thank you."

Cat watched as he shut the door behind him. She crept to the window to see the men still looking for people to interrogate. Oh, a pox on them for it. At this rate, they'd be stuck here forever.

But better here than in a German palace. Keeping that thought close, she quickly poured water in a basin and used the small cloth there to freshen up. She was still touched by Lochlan's kindness at purchasing her the gowns. Then again, it only made sense, really. He was used to looking after other people. As the laird it was his job to anticipate the needs and wants of his people and to meet them as best he could.

At least that was the theory, but most of the men she'd met in such jobs had developed the attitude that whatever was best for them must be the best for all.

Kneeling, she opened his saddlebags to look for his brush. It was extremely neat. Every item was carefully wrapped and placed. Poor man to need even something as innocuous as this to be so proper.

"I must be making him insane."

The only order she subscribed to was that of whimsy and imp. In fact, it was taking all of her willpower not to scramble the contents a bit just to see his reaction. But she owed him too much for that.

She forced herself to brush out her hair, then return the brush to the exact spot where he'd placed it . . . oh very well, she moved it. It was hard for her to not have a bit of fun with him.

As soon as she was finished, she opened the door to tell him to reenter. No sooner had she done so than she realized what a mistake she'd made.

For there in the hallway stood Myles.

Chapter 4

Myles's beady eyes lit up the moment they focused on her. "Good evening, Catarina. It's so nice to see you again."

Cat looked at Lochlan, unsure of how to respond.

Before she could even blink, Lochlan had Myles by the scruff of his neck and was shoving him through the door. She stumbled back into the room and shut the door while Lochlan held a knife to Myles's throat.

"Don't speak," Lochlan warned him. "Any word will get you killed, do you understand?"

He nodded.

"We don't have anything to tie him with," Cat whispered.

"You should know you can't escape us. There's—"

Lochlan silenced him with a hard punch to his jaw. Myles's eyes rolled back in his head before he hit the floor with a loud thump.

Cat arched a brow at Lochlan, who was frowning down at Myles.

"Not quite death, but at least it got him to shut up, eh?"

He quickly gathered their things.

"What if he wakes up?"

"Then we're going to be chased, so let's not dally, shall we?"

She followed him from the room and down to the stable, where he hastily retrieved their horses. Just as they were mounted, a cry rent the air.

"The princess is with the Scotsman. Stop her!"

Lochlan cursed. "Can you keep up with me, lass?"

"Are you jesting? To avoid them I could beat the devil himself and all his disciples." She set her heels to the horse. Neighing, it tore from the stable.

Lochlan smiled at her spirit and skill as he set his horse after hers. He was unfamiliar with this land, which put them at a great disadvantage. The horses had rested a bit, but he wasn't sure how long they could last at a full run. With any luck, the guards' horses would be tired as well.

If not, this was going to be a short, and fatal, escape.

As they left the stable area, several of the guards lunged at them while others tried to block their path. Lochlan and Catarina dodged them and flew toward the edge of town. He could hear the commotion of the men scrambling for horses.

"Keep your head down," he told Catarina. "Continue north and don't stop whatever you do." He only hoped that the darkness would be kind enough to shield them from the guards and not so cruel as to hide a deep rut or dip in the ground that would send one of them flying from their mount.

The last time he'd been chased like this, it'd been his father on his tail, drunk, trying to kill him. Only then Lochlan had known the countryside like the back of his hand. He'd avoided his father easily enough and spent the night in a cave, high above their lands. In the morning, he'd awakened with a nasty cold, which hadn't kept his father from beating him.

You're a worthless bastard. If not for the fact your

mother lacked all backbone, I'd swear you were whelped from another man's loins.

It was an insult so common that Lochlan had practically cut his teeth on it. He didn't even know what made him think of it now. But one thing was certain . . . if they caught him, they wouldn't come away from the battle without scars of their own.

Grinding his teeth, he urged his horse faster.

Cat's heart was pounding as they tore through the darkness. She hated not being able to see. It was a moonless night, which would help conceal them from the guards, but it didn't help them find the road they should be traveling on. A twinge of fear crept through her and she hated that. She didn't like being afraid. But the darkness was oppressive.

Suddenly, Lochlan was beside her, slowing her down.

"Is something wrong?"

He motioned her to silence.

She didn't speak, but the thrumming of her heart in her ears was deafening.

Lochlan slid to the ground and held his hands up for her to join him. Not sure if she should obey, she forced herself to trust him. His grip was sure as he guided her to land by his side. He slapped the rump of her horse and sent it off and running.

"What are—"

"Sh!" he snapped.

Angry, she watched as he led his horse to the side of the road and had it lie down. He covered it with leaves and debris, then had her lie by its side. As soon as she was covered, he joined her. He'd barely covered himself before she heard the thundering sound of approaching hooves.

"Do you see them?" one of the guards shouted.

"Aye. They're still running ahead."

As soon as they passed, she started to rise only to have Lochlan hold her down. She could feel the muscles of his arm flexing intimately against her stomach and breasts. Just as she opened her mouth to protest, she heard another rider approaching. She actually gaped at the sound and waited for it to pass.

Once it'd long faded, Lochlan pushed himself up, then extended his hand toward her.

"How did you know there would be another rider?"

"Any commander with half a brain will have one riding in the back, just in case of this ruse." He swung her onto the back of his horse before he joined her.

"Can your horse carry both of us?"

He urged his horse to the east. "For a bit. We'll

have to travel slower than before, but since they're not at our heels, we should be fine."

"Unless they realize my horse carries no rider."

"Hopefully by that time, they'll be far enough gone that they won't be able to backtrack to find us easily."

Cat hoped he was right. The last thing she wanted was to return to her father in chains. Not to mention, Lochlan was putting his own life in danger by helping her. He owed her nothing and yet he was being kinder to her than her own family. It made her heart soften toward him.

"Have I told you just how much I appreciate what you're doing for me?"

"Nay, lass, you've only insulted me."

"Then I shall never insult you again . . . even should you deserve it."

Lochlan was taken aback by the tenderness in her voice. More used to venom than honey from people, he wasn't sure how to respond. "Thank you."

"You're quite welcome."

They continued on in silence as Lochlan kept an ear attuned for any sound or sign of the guards' return. But as they made their way through the forest, it appeared they'd managed to evade the guards.

Cat listened intently for any telltale sign of the

guards' return, too, but after a little while the stress, rhythm of the horse's gait, and the warmth of Lochlan's body lulled her to sleepiness. She found herself melting into his body.

Goodness, the man smelled so good. The scent of his skin was pleasant and masculine. It made her want to rub herself against him, but she could never do something like that. Still, the desire burned through her even as her eyelids were becoming heavier and heavier.

She tried her best to stay awake, but it had been a long day, and she'd been running, literally, since she first snuck out of bed. Now that she felt safe, her exhaustion was taking over.

Lochlan frowned as he felt Catarina falling asleep. Her body relaxed so suddenly that it was all he could do to maintain his hold on her. He stopped the horse long enough to shift her weight in his arms before he renewed his course.

He held her carefully, amazed that she'd trusted him enough to sleep. There was something about her that was very hard-edged. It was obvious that she'd been around as many false friends as he had. People who only wanted to be close to him because they wanted something from him, either power or coin. Or they just wanted to brag that they knew the laird.

His father had warned him of such people, but as a young man he'd assumed his father was jaded and bitter. The fact that his father had known the truth of it burned inside him. He'd learned his lessons the hard way and he wondered who had hurt Catarina in that manner.

But unlike him, she was still open. She didn't shield herself from the world. She kept herself out there, exposed, as if she'd rather have the pain than not. He couldn't even begin to understand that. He'd had enough pain dealt to him against his will, the last thing he wanted was to invite anymore into his house.

You can't help people, boy. They're all users. They take what they want with no regard for you. Give me a coin, they'll beg and the moment you do, they slide a blade between your ribs to take the rest from you. Trust me. People are the fleas infecting and sullying the fur of God's creation.

He'd never wanted to believe that, but there were times when he feared his father was more right than wrong. And as he held Catarina, he wondered what she'd do to betray him.

He flinched as he saw an image of Maire's face in his mind. She'd been so beautiful and unspoiled. To touch even her hand had been like touching divinity.

And she'd ripped his heart out and spat on it. Just as his father had predicted, she'd cast him aside for a bigger catch. Just as Isobail had done with his brothers.

Catarina needed him to help her. But if ever given the chance, he had no doubt she'd throw him to the wolves and laugh as she did so. It wouldn't even be her fault. It was just the nature of humanity. One didn't nurse a viper at the bosom unless one expected it to bite.

His best course of action was to get her to her family and be done with her. The sooner she was away from him, the sooner he could return to his own business.

And yet as he stared down at her serene face and remembered the taste of her lips, he wondered what it would be like to have a woman like this by his side. His brothers had all been fortunate enough to find women worth dying for. Women who'd proven themselves loyal and loving.

But he would never be so fortunate. There was no use in dreaming of anything better. He was laird and his life was to serve his people. That would be enough for him.

Even so, it was hard not to imagine a woman like Catarina holding him close. She would be a fierce mother. Unlike his own, she wouldn't cower before her husband, then take out her abuse on a child. Catarina would fight tooth and nail to protect her own and most likely anyone else who was weak. He admired that.

Not to mention she was beautiful. Not in a classic sense, but in a very exotic way. Her dark hair and eyes reminded him of a devilish feline. Her skin was tanned and dark, unlike the guarded complexions of most ladies. He could just imagine her running barefoot through a meadow, laughing as she did so.

Lochlan paused in his consideration as he heard a sharp noise to his right. Reining the horse, he listened carefully.

Had the guards found them?

Just as he was certain he'd imagined the sound, something went whizzing past his face. The arrow embedded in a tree to his left. Lochlan reached for his sword.

"Careful, my friend. Pull that out and it'll be the last mistake of your life."

Chapter 5

Lochlan debated long enough for them to let fly another arrow.

"This isn't a game. Back your hand from your hilt, or the next shot will be through your head."

Clenching his teeth in anger that they'd gotten the drop on him, Lochlan did as ordered even though it galled him to the core of his soul. If he were alone, he might be able to fight them. But with Catarina asleep in his arms, he didn't have any choice except to comply.

A tall, gawky youth around the age of ten and five came forward to jerk his sword from its sheath. As he did so, his light gray eyes fell to Catarina's sleeping form and he gasped audibly before stepping back. "Bracken . . . there's something here you'll wish to see."

"I've seen plenty of swords in my time, boy."

"Aye, but 'tis not the sword you'll recognize. He holds Princess Catarina."

How did the boy know that? Lochlan scowled at the words as a man near his own age came out from behind a tree. With long black hair and eyes so light they appeared translucent, he held a longbow with a nocked arrow. Lean, but still well muscled, there was no doubt this man would be quick and lethal in a fight. Even so, Lochlan knew he could take him.

The man approached cautiously until he was able to peer over Lochlan's arm to see Catarina. The instant he could see her face, he aimed the arrow toward Lochlan's head again. "What are you doing with her?"

"That would be none of your business."

The man's eyes narrowed dangerously. "Cat!" he shouted in a tone that sent several birds into flight. "Wake yourself."

She jerked awake so fast, her head bumped into Lochlan's jaw. He cursed in response to the sharp pain as she rubbed her temple.

Her gaze was irritable and accusatory. "Why did you yell at me?"

"It wasn't me." He indicated the two men below with a jerk of his chin. "They're the ones who disturbed your slumber."

She frowned until her gaze focused on the man's face, then she looked incredulous. "Bracken of Ravenglass?"

His features softened instantly. "Aye, love. Now tell me if I needs shoot this man or not."

Her frown returned. "Shoot who?"

"The one holding you."

She laughed. "Lochlan? He's not holding me . . ." She hesitated as she glanced down to see Lochlan's arms around her. "I mean, aye, he's holding me, but not as you mean. He's a friend."

Lochlan wasn't sure if she realized the fact that as she said those words, she ran her hand affectionately up his arm, over his biceps. His entire body ignited and by the scowl on Bracken's face, it was obvious he noted her action as well and didn't care for it in the least.

Bracken lowered his arrow, then gave a low whistle. As he did so, another youth came forward. At first it appeared to be another male, but as the form drew closer, Lochlan realized it was a very slender woman dressed in a brown leather jerkin and breeches. Like the other two, she had black hair that was braided down her back and pale blue eyes like Bracken.

Cat stiffened in his arms. "Julia? Bryce? What are you doing here? Dressed like *that*?"

Bracken looked down to the bow in his hands before he spoke in a sarcastic tone. "It appears assaulting your friend. I suppose some things never change."

Again Catarina laughed. "I would expect no less from the likes of you. But why are you here in France?"

"We"—he indicated the other two along with himself—"are outlaws. If I return to England, King Henry will demand our lives."

"What? I don't understand."

Bracken sighed before he put the arrow in the quiver that was slung over his back and draped the bow over the opposite shoulder. "My father took up with the wrong sort and was denounced as a traitor. Our lands were confiscated along with my armor and horses, my father was executed, and we were offered the choice between banishment or beheadedment. Obviously, we chose the former."

Lochlan snorted. It was rare for that choice ever

to be given. Usually the king's justice was extremely swift and final. "Henry must have been in a good mood that day."

Bracken sneered. "If you say so."

Catarina ignored the ice and venom in Bracken's voice. Not that she blamed him for it. He was more than entitled to his hostility over such an injustice. "So you're just traveling about now?"

Bracken shrugged. "There wasn't much choice in the matter, so we took a page from your book. I mean, I have tried to find work, but no one wants to hire a disgraced nobleman whose only experience is on a tourney field. I don't even know how they can tell what I am. I never mention it to them when I ask for work. It's as if they can smell it on me somehow."

Not really. There was an imperious bearing to the man that no one could mistake. Not to mention his French was formal and tinged with an English accent. 'Twould be obvious to anyone that this man was more at home running the town than working in it.

Catarina glanced down at Bryce who still held Lochlan's sword in his hands. "Why did you stop us?"

Bracken gave her a devilish grin. "I was planning to rob you."

Catarina shook her head and tsked at him. "You've taken to thievery?"

"Better than hungry."

She cast a chiding stare at all three of them. "I am so disappointed in you, Bracken."

"You don't understand, Cat," Julia said defensively. "Bracken hasn't eaten in three days. He's been giving his portions to us and still we're all starving. If Bracken doesn't eat soon—"

"Enough, Julia," Bracken said between clenched teeth. "She doesn't need the sordid details of our lives."

Lochlan opened his saddlebags with one hand and tossed a small wrapped parcel to Julia. "'Tis meat and bread for you."

Her eyes lit up instantly. "God bless you."

He inclined his head to her, then tossed a small bag to Bryce. The youth opened it to find several gold marks.

Bracken cursed as he saw it, then snatched it from Bryce's hands. He stalked toward them with his eyes snapping fury. "We don't need charity."

Lochlan arched a brow at his untoward behavior as he refused to take the coins back. "But you were going to steal it?"

"I would have *earned* it that way."

While he might fault the man's reasoning, he

could almost respect it. He didn't like taking anything himself unless he earned it either. "Fine then, ride with us and consider that payment. We're being chased by the king's men and I'm trying to reach a tourney in Rouen. I could use an extra pair of hands to fight should the guards find us again."

Bracken scowled at him. "Why are you running?"

"My father wishes me to marry."

He looked as aghast as Lochlan must have the first time he'd heard her say that. "Would that be so bad?"

Catarina stiffened. "For me, aye. And well you know it. Now if you don't mind, we needs be on our way. With you, or without you."

Lochlan was amused to know she didn't reserve that imperious tone strictly for him. It was nice to see it directed at someone else for a change.

Bracken hesitated before he turned his head to Julia. "Fetch the horses."

She let out a delighted squeak before she ran to get them while Bryce returned the sword to Lochlan.

"Sorry," the boy said before he retreated to Bracken's side.

In no time the three of them were mounted and

all of them were back on the road. Bryce and Julia shared the meat while they rode.

Bracken refused, saying he'd rather see them full. Instead, he rode abreast of Lochlan while the other two followed behind. "How many guards are in pursuit?"

"Around a score."

"Good number that."

Lochlan didn't respond to his sarcasm.

Julia galloped her horse to Bracken's side and again held out the meat to her brother. "Please eat something. You're going to be ill if you keep going without food."

"She's right," Lochlan said. "We'll stop in the morning for supplies."

He could see the reservation in Bracken's eyes and he admired the man's loyalty to his siblings and his sacrifice on their behalf.

"Please, Bracken. I can't stand the thought of losing you, too."

That small plea must have weakened his resolve. Bracken took a small portion. "Now you eat the rest and quit pestering me."

She offered her older brother a bright smile. "Very well, Lord Churlish." Then she fell back to ride beside Bryce.

Bracken swallowed the meat before he turned

his attention back to Lochlan. "I still don't know who you are."

"Lochlan MacAllister."

"He's their laird," Catarina added.

Bracken averted his gaze. "I see." His tone was empty and yet speculative.

Catarina cast a frown at Lochlan before she looked to Bracken. "What do you mean by that?"

"Nothing."

"Lochlan, what does he mean by that?"

As if he had a clue. But he was curious enough himself to pursue it. "By your tone, I can tell there's more to that statement. Don't worry about offending me. I have four brothers who tutored me well on patience."

Bracken glanced back at Bryce as if he understood completely before he spoke again. "I met your father a couple of times when I was a young squire at Henry's court."

With those few words, total clarity was his. "Ah."

Bracken nodded. "Exactly."

Cat stared back at forth as the two of them appeared to be speaking in code to one another and she wanted to be let in on this great secret. "What does that mean?"

"Nothing," they said in unison.

Cat rolled her eyes at them. "Men," she said to Julia. "They are ever a blight on our gender."

Julia giggled as she licked her fingers.

Letting out a frustrated sigh, she returned her attention to the men. "So what is this he met your father that brings mutual understanding to the two of you?"

Lochlan gave her a gimlet glare. "You're not going to allow me peace from this are you?"

"Not until I have an answer."

"Fine. My father had a bit of a reputation at the English court."

"Reputation for what?"

"Cruelty."

"Oh," she whispered, feeling guilty now that she'd pursued the issue. "I'm sorry, Lochlan, I shouldn't have pressed."

"It's fine, lass. It isn't as if it's a secret." He indicated Bracken with a tilt of his head. "Many people are well aware of what my father was."

Even so, she shouldn't have pried. Such things were personal and no doubt he had scars from the experience. If his father was cruel to strangers, then he was most likely the same way to his family and that made her ache for him as she wondered what other secrets Lochlan kept locked inside himself.

They all fell quiet as they traveled in the darkness. Cat listened to the rustle of the wind through the trees. There was a bit of a chill to the air, but the close proximity of Lochlan's body chased it away. The scent of him and feel of his muscles around her went a long way in keeping her warm, too.

Lochlan stiffened, in more ways than one, as Catarina laid her hand on his arm before she tucked her head under his chin and relaxed against him again. Even though it was a purely platonic touch, there was something so intimate about it that his blood fired.

But the worst was that it awakened a longing inside him that he'd never felt before. He'd never really been at ease around women. They were too conniving and fragile for his liking. He didn't like tears or melodrama, and they seemed to bring an abundance of both. Case in point, his quest had been frustrating but peaceful until Catarina crossed his path. Not once had he pulled his sword out or had anyone shoot an arrow at his head.

The minute she came into his life—chaos.

Yet the sensation of her in his arms . . . it was heaven. And he found himself wondering what it would be like to have a wife. To have someone who could tease him and who wouldn't make him uncomfortable by wondering what game she played or how she was conniving to win his hand.

His sisters-in-law were perfect matches for his brothers. They treated them with respect and loved them in a way he'd never thought possible. Each one had literally saved his brothers' lives.

Surely he deserved as much? But as soon as that thought went through him, he silently scoffed as he remembered his father's bitter words. *Deserving has nothing to do with anything, boy. Get that out your head. The world owes you nothing and I owe you even less.*

His father was right. If deserving had anything to do with anything, his brother Sin would have been laird. Sin was the eldest, not Lochlan. But his father had never claimed Sin and where was the justice in that?

Nay, life wasn't about justice and earning a future. It was about negotiating and taking charge.

Even so, it took all his willpower not to rub his cheek against her hair and savor the softness of it on his skin. Images of her naked in his arms tormented him. It would be so easy to place his lips on her throat . . .

Stop. Any more and he might very well turn mad from the heat in his body. She was a cousin of his sister-in-law who had saved Ewan's life. As such, he would protect and honor her. There would be nothing more than that.

Bracken rode up beside him. "Is she asleep again?"

Lochlan glanced down to see she was completely relaxed against him. "I think so."

"Interesting. I've never known her to trust anyone except Bavel that way."

Yet she didn't seem to hesitate collapsing against him. It was odd and almost insulting that he bored her to such a state that she constantly fell asleep around him. He didn't normally elicit such a response from anyone. Most people were extremely reserved in his presence.

"How long have you known her?" he asked Bracken.

He smiled as if the memory warmed him. "We met as children, here in France. Paris actually. I'd come here with my father and was at court, and she was visiting her father that summer." Amusement radiated from his eyes. "She was livid at being forced to stay in the palace and made to wear finery. Every few minutes, she'd kick off her shoes and tear the wimple and veil from her hair. She said she was suffocating from the weight of her gown. I thought her poor nurse would have apoplexy from dealing with her."

Lochlan could just imagine her tantrum. "Her father tolerated it?"

The humor fled from his face. "Not a bit. They would whip her and she would laugh, even while there were tears in her eyes from the pain. 'You can't make me wear it,' she'd say bravely. 'You can beat me until I turn blue, but you'll never make me wear it.'"

"Why didn't they give in to her and just let her be?"

"Prince Philip? Now king?" Bracken asked incredulously. "Do you honestly think he'd ever cede any point, especially to a willful child?"

It was true. Philip was known for his iron will and inflexibility. The only opinion that ever mattered was his own. "So what happened?"

"Her uncle stole her away in the middle of the night and took her back to her mother. After that, they left their home and traveled about so that her father could never again command her back to his lands and her station."

That had been a daring move on their part. It was a wonder Philip hadn't dragged them back to Paris in chains. "I wonder how he found her this time?"

"There's no telling. But I doubt she went to him voluntarily."

Lochlan smiled at the understatement. "You seem to know each other rather well for people who only met once as children."

Bracken gave him a pointed look. "Is that jealousy I hear in your voice?"

"Hardly. I barely know her myself."

Still suspicion hung heavy on Bracken's brow. "Since my father knew and liked her mother greatly, he extended an invitation to them to come stay with us during our annual spring festival. For years, they would visit and stay at least a month at our castle in England."

Now there was a prickling of jealousy inside him. There were years of history between the two of them. He didn't know why that one fact bothered him, but it did. "No wonder you know her well then."

"Not as well as I think you mean. Cat has no interest in being tied to any man and she never has. She values her freedom more than any person I've ever known."

But the life of a gypsy was no life for a princess. Traveling with no real home and having been alienated from her father must have been hard on her and her mother. He couldn't imagine the hardships they must have faced.

Bracken cleared his throat. "I'm surprised you haven't asked me of my lands and titles."

Lochlan gave him a sheepish glance. "I thought it might be a sore spot best left undisturbed."

"Aye, it is. Can you imagine losing everything in the blink of an eye?"

Lochlan looked over his shoulder at Bryce and Julia. In his opinion, Bracken hadn't lost everything—he still had quite a bit with him. "Aye, I can. I've lost one of my brothers."

Bracken crossed himself. "Then you know what I mean. My deepest condolences."

"And mine to you as well for your father."

Bracken inclined his head to him in mutual respect before he let his horse drift behind so that he could ride abreast of his siblings. Lochlan looked down at Catarina, who had one hand tucked none too comfortably against his groin while the other rested in her own lap. Her perfect lips were parted and if they'd been alone, he wasn't too sure he wouldn't have sampled them.

But with the others nearby . . . It would only be a fantasy of his. Dear God, she was beautiful in his arms. . . .

They rode in silence for the rest of the night. It wasn't until daybreak that they found themselves approaching a small farm.

Bracken came abreast of his horse again. "Have you any more coin?"

"Aye."

"Then let us see if the farmer would mind putting us up in his barn for a bit. What say you?"

Lochlan had to stifle a yawn. "I couldn't agree more. Sleep would be most welcome at this point." He handed Bracken a few coins.

Bracken rode ahead while they stayed back so as not to frighten the farmer or his family. Generally the sight of so many nobles at a French peasant's home boded ill and they were ever on their guard against foul play.

After a few minutes, Bracken returned with a leg of salted lamb, a jug of mead, and two loaves of bread. "We can sleep in the barn so long as we don't disturb their animals."

Lochlan snorted. "I don't plan to disturb anything more than the hay as I lay myself upon it."

"I hear you." Bracken passed the meat and bread to his siblings.

Julia paused as she started to tear a piece. She held the loaf out toward him. "Would you like a bit to eat, Lord Lochlan?"

"Just call me Lochlan, my lady, and I'll pass. You eat your fill."

He saw the gratitude in her eyes before she tore her loaf in half and gave it back to Bracken. Lochlan watched as Bracken walked away from them to eat it, but he didn't miss the way the man tore into the bread like a starving beggar. He ate it so quickly that Lochlan was amazed he didn't chew his own fingers in the process.

Sympathy for them welled up inside him. No one deserved the misery that had been dealt to them. They appeared to be decent enough people. All they needed was a chance.

"You know, Bracken," he said as he joined him, "I can always use another trained knight in my company."

Bracken scoffed as he remounted his horse and led them toward the barn. "I have no sword or armor. I only have a horse because I stole mine back from the king's own company. What good would I be to you?"

"Retaking what belongs to you is no crime in my book. The offer stands. Armor and swords can be bought."

Suspicion clouded Bracken's eyes. "Why would you do such a thing?"

Lochlan met his gaze levelly as he struggled to keep the pain out of his voice and eyes. "Because no son should be held accountable for the actions of his father. Nor should he be judged by them."

Bracken gave him a hard stare and Lochlan

was sure the man understood that he was talking about his own father as well as Bracken's. "What of my siblings?"

"You'll need a squire. Bryce appears to be of age for such and my mother would be most delighted to have a young lady to train and dote upon."

Bracken glanced to Julia and the love and relief in his eyes was almost tangible. It was obvious he'd been more than concerned about her welfare on the road. Even so, he wasn't about to subject them to complete charity. "We will pay our way."

"Of that I have no doubt."

Bracken held his arm out to him. "Then I'm your man."

Keeping Catarina cradled against him, Lochlan shook his arm and nodded. "Welcome to the Mac-Allister clan."

Tears glistened in Julia's eyes. "We have a home again? Truly?"

"Aye, love," Bracken said, his voice breaking. "It appears we do."

She let out a squeal before she ran to Bryce and hugged him. "Did you hear that, brother? We have a home!"

"I heard until you screamed in my ear. Now I fear I shall never hear again."

She shoved playfully at him. "Oh shush, Lord Grump. You're just as excited as I am and you know it."

A small smile from the moody adolescent confirmed it before he mumbled under his breath and walked away.

Bracken held Lochlan's horse while he slid to the ground with Catarina in his arms. She didn't even stir. "I swear this woman could sleep through most anything."

"Aye. She'd be the perfect mate for a man who snores."

Lochlan laughed. "True enough." He carried Catarina into the barn, where Julia quickly made a makeshift pallet for her. Laying her down, he covered her with his cloak. Her cheeks were bright from her slumber and her black hair coiled becomingly around her face. Damn, but she was the most beautiful woman he'd ever seen, especially when she was silent and not tormenting him.

Bracken paused beside him. "You keep staring at her like that, and I'm going to suspect you're infatuated with her."

He scoffed at Bracken's words. "I'm too old for infatuation."

"We're never too old for infatuation."

Of course they were. He was a man full grown

and would soon be married to another . . . if he ever got back and proposed. Infatuations were for children and silly women, not men.

Disregarding Bracken's words, he went to unsaddle his horse and make it as comfortable as possible while Bracken and Bryce tended theirs. Julia made the pallets, then went instantly to sleep.

Bryce was next to follow her, then Bracken. As he followed them, Lochlan made sure to take his sword to the pallet with him. He placed himself between Bryce and Catarina on the floor. Cradling the blade to his side, he closed his eyes and was instantly asleep.

But even so, dreams of Catarina tormented him. He could see and hear her laughing with him, feel her body against his. It was the most pleasurable thought imaginable. Oh to have her with him like that forever . . .

Impossible thoughts those. She was a woman who refused to be tied down and he was a man whose restraints were never to be broken. He couldn't travel about. He had too many duties and responsibilities for such frivolity.

But his dreams didn't care about that. Here, he was free to be with her and, honestly, it was a sweet moment that left him smiling even in his sleep.

* * *

Cat woke up to a foreign noise. Still exhausted, she opened one eye to find herself enveloped by a warm body. Her back was against someone's chest while one heavy masculine arm held her close. Even the backs of her thighs rested against his.

A quick survey of the barn to see Bracken lying asleep a few feet from her told her exactly who held her. Lochlan. A smile curled her lips as she tilted her head up to see him sound asleep over her.

Goodness, he was a handsome man. The stubble on his face seemed so out of place and at the same time it added a wildness to him that was absolutely compelling. She wondered if he even knew he held her like this. Given the rigidity of his personality, she doubted it.

He must have reached out to her in his sleep. Good thing that since Bryce was only a few inches from them. No doubt Lochlan would have been most horrified to be curled up against the boy.

Smiling at the thought, she impulsively laced her fingers with his. His hand was so much larger than hers that it amazed her. His fingers were long and well tapered. Meticulously clean and strong. He had a small gold signet ring on his smallest finger. It was engraved with the MacAllister crest of a lion and thistle.

As she turned it slightly on his finger, she again heard the sound that had awakened her. It was a group of horses.

She tensed and waited to see how close they would come. They stopped not far from the barn. But her relief was short-lived as she heard a man's gruff voice.

"Ho, good farmer. We're searching for someone."

Chapter 6

Cat sat up immediately and shook Lochlan awake. She covered his mouth with her hand as he started to speak and motioned for him to listen.

"Who are you seeking, sir?"

"The worst sort of miscreant. He calls himself Le Faucon and is traveling with two boys. His brothers, we believe."

"Ah, nay, sir. We've seen no such persons here."

"Are you sure? The crown is offering quite a reward for any information that leads to the arrest of this thief."

"Then I most certainly wish to claim it, but unfortunately, he's never been seen here."

"Very well. Should you hear of anything—"

"I won't hesitate to let the local sheriff know."

"Good day to you then."

"Good day, sir."

Cat didn't breathe again until she heard the men ride off. She offered Lochlan a sheepish smile. "I'm sorry I woke you. I thought it was more pressing than it turned out to be."

"Nay, lass. You did well. It could have been dire indeed." He scratched at the stubble on his chin. "You should probably wake the others so that we can be on our way. The next group that comes calling could very well be seeking us."

She didn't like the sound of that, but knew he was most likely right. Scrambling away from him, she quickly did as he asked.

Bracken groaned as soon as she poked his shoulder to wake him. "Have kindness for me, Cat. Slide a blade between my ribs and leave me here to sleep."

She shoved playfully at him. "Get up, you louse. The daylight's wasting."

He harrumphed at her. "You're an evil shrew. Unlike someone I could name, I didn't spend half the night sleeping in a man's arms."

"I didn't know you had such fantasies, Bracken. I don't know if Lochlan would concur, but—"

"Don't you even . . ." he snapped, rising immediately. He gave Lochlan an indignant grimace. "Did you hear her, Lochlan? I'm not sure which of us was most insulted."

His eyes actually twinkled. "I think her insult was definitely directed toward you."

"You would," Bracken grumbled as he made his way out of the stable.

Julia laughed at her brother's surliness. "Never mind him. He's always disagreeable whenever he wakes."

"'Tis true," Bryce concurred before he yawned. "Father used to say that if our castle was ever breached, he hoped the invaders broke into Bracken's room while he slept. Then he'd be like a berserker and defeat them all just to have a few moments more of rest."

Cat smiled even though a part of her ached at the tale. She remembered their father—tall like Bracken, he'd been a kind, gentle man and she couldn't imagine how he'd ever been labeled a traitor. The loss of him would have to weigh tragically on all three of them. It made her heart ache.

After Bracken's return, she and Julia went to attend their needs while the men readied the horses. By the angle of the sun in the sky, she'd guess it was just before midday. All in all, she felt rested—Lochlan had made an excellent cushion in the night. But it was late in the day to start their journey. She only hoped that the others weren't exhausted.

The two of them knelt on the ground to wash their faces in a small stream. Cat shook her head as she remembered what had awakened her. "Julia? Have you ever heard of a thief called Faucon?"

The girl actually paled. "Why do you ask?"

"That was what woke me. I heard a group of men asking the farmer about him and I was wondering if you'd heard of him in your journeys."

Cat wouldn't have believed it possible had she not seen it, but Julia actually paled even more. She sprang to her feet and rushed back to the barn.

She hurried after her, wondering what was up. By the time she entered the barn, Julia had Bracken by his arm.

"Bracken, we must hurry."

He frowned at his sister before he disentangled his arm from her grasp. "Why?"

"Cat said there were men here, seeking you."

He cursed.

Cat scowled at them as she finally understood what was going on. "You're Faucon?"

There was no pride in his face, only a look of deep resignation. "Aye, indeed. And don't look at me like that, Cat. You've been taken care of all your life. You have no idea what it's like to bear the responsibility of a loved one's belly and health. Trust me. It makes you do things you would never think yourself capable of."

"Hunger has no morals," Lochlan said quietly.

She saw the relief in Bracken's eyes as he realized he was in the presence of someone who wouldn't judge him for what he'd done to protect his siblings. Cat was trying hard not to. But she'd been taught from the cradle that it was better to starve to death than to take even a morsel from someone else to feed herself.

However, her morals had never been tested and she knew Bracken to be a fair and decent man. If he had stolen, then truly he would have had no other recourse.

Cat offered him an understanding smile. "I don't condemn you for what you've done, Bracken. I'm just hurt that you've been reduced to this."

His eyes burned into her. "Believe me, no one is sadder over it than I am."

Cat stepped forward and hugged him. "You're a good man, Bracken and well I know it. Have no fear that I think any less of you."

"Thank you," he whispered before he stepped away from her as if embarrassed by her actions.

"We just have to make sure no one recognizes him." Lochlan opened his saddlebags and pulled out two of his tunics. "It'll be a bit large for Bryce, but you should find it a good fit."

Cat noted the way Bracken ran his hand over the fine linen. She could tell that the man had never thought to touch its like again. No one would mistake them for peasants or thieves wearing those garments.

Taking a cue from Lochlan, she fished one of her gowns out and handed it to Julia, who beamed like a child on a Christmas Day feast.

"'Tis lovely! Thank you, Cat, thank you."

She inclined her head to the girl, who practically ran for privacy so that she could change her clothes while her brothers exchanged their tunics immediately. Cat averted her gaze, but the flash of Bracken's well-muscled chest made her think about Lochlan's. How strange that was what her desire would be directed to and not at the beautiful body before her. Rather it was the man to her left that she wanted to see naked.

You have lost your mind.

Truly, there was no other explanation. Why else would she not be fascinated by the swell of Bracken's muscles? He was a fine-looking man and yet his body, while she could appreciate it, didn't make her heart pound or steal her breath away. What she needed was something to distract her from these disturbing thoughts.

"I'll see about buying more food from the farmer," she said, moving toward the door.

Lochlan stopped her and handed her his purse. "You'll find your purchase much easier if you have coin."

She laughed, trying to cover her embarrassment. "This is probably true. My thanks."

A slight hint of a smile tugged at the edge of his lips and at her heart. She didn't know how such a simple gesture could make her knees weak when Bracken's nudity had done nothing to her, but it did.

Yet that was nothing compared to the overwhelming urge she had to reach up and touch his face. Afraid of the mere thought, she quickly took her leave.

Lochlan couldn't help but watch as Catarina sashayed out of the barn. There was something about the sway of her hips what was beguiling.

"You've fallen bad."

He frowned at Bracken's words. "I've what?"

"You know what. If her father were here, he'd gouge out your eyes for the way you're staring after her. You're all but salivating."

Lochlan felt a childish urge to argue, but to what point? Bracken was right. He hadn't felt this kind of pull toward a woman in many years. "Aye, well, I'm old enough to know when not to act."

"Would it be so bad if you did?"

Aye, it would. He had enough responsibility on him and Catarina wasn't the kind of woman he needed in his life. Her willful spirit would be a constant strain on any man.

"Hearts are fickle things," he said quietly to Bracken. "'Tis why the Lord gave us brains so that we may recognize stupidity when we see it. She's a French princess whose father already has her husband chosen. I learned a long time ago to stay out of such politics. I've had one clan war that almost destroyed my people. I've no wish to start another."

"Then why are you helping her?"

Lochlan looked away as he tightened the cinch for his saddle. "I owe her my brother's life and I gave her my word."

"Is that the only reason?"

"Of course it is."

Bracken tsked at him. "If you choose to believe those lies . . ."

Julia scoffed at her brother as she returned to

their side. "Look at you . . . preaching to another about love." She shook her head. "Pay him no attention, Lord Lochlan. My brother knows even less of love than I do."

Bracken rolled his eyes at her. "You've listened to too many minstrels, child."

"Perhaps, but I would never suffer the one I love to marry another."

There was no mistaking the fury her words ignited inside Bracken. His eyes blazing, he moved to saddle their horses.

Lochlan frowned at his sudden departure and at the pain that marked Julia's brow.

"I should better counsel my tongue," she said in a contrite tone. "I wouldn't have hurt him for anything."

Having wounded his own brothers on many occasions without malice intended, he completely understood her. "We all make such mistakes."

"Aye, but the loss of Jacqueline still plagues him and well I know it. It was thoughtless of me to remind him of her."

"If that be the case, lass, I'm not the one who should hear your apology."

She nodded before she made her way over to Bracken, who greeted her with a stern glower. But as soon as she apologized, he drew her into a hug and kissed the top of her head before he released her.

Still, the pain in his eyes lingered. It was obvious that Bracken did indeed mourn the loss of this Jacqueline. Yet another reason for Lochlan to guard his heart. Emotions weakened a man and he had no desire to be laid low by something as insignificant as the mere touch of a woman.

But as Catarina returned to the barn he found that resolve tested. And when she caught his gaze and smiled at him, the strange fluttering in his stomach told him that he was all but lost.

It's just lust.

He'd felt that bitter sting in his loins many times in his life. One woman's body could soothe that itch just as well as another.

But in his heart, he knew better. Love mattered greatly and he had no wish for any woman save Catarina.

Bracken cleared his throat to draw Lochlan's attention to him. "We're going to need another horse."

Lochlan nodded. "I agree, but there's not one here. I suggest we try to find one as soon as possible though. I've been riding mine rather hard for the last fortnight."

"As have we," Bracken said.

Catarina looked back and forth between them. "I would volunteer to walk, but it would slow us down."

Bracken snorted at the mere prospect. "As if either of us would ride and allow you to walk." He rolled his eyes at her before he spoke to Lochlan. "The women should ride together. It'll be less taxing on a single steed."

Logically, Lochlan concurred. But he felt a small twinge at the thought of her riding with Julia and not him. Pushing that thought aside, he took a bit of bread from Catarina's hand before he helped Julia mount her horse.

Catarina passed out the rest of the loaf before he helped her up behind Julia. Then she shared bread with Julia while he mounted.

"How well do you know this countryside?" he asked Bracken.

"Well enough."

"Then I need you to take us to Rouen. Do you know the way?"

"Aye, it's two days west of here."

Lochlan let out a relieved breath that it was so close. That would put them there near the end of the tourney, but Stryder should still be in attendance. It was the best he could have hoped for. "Then let's not tarry."

Bracken led the way from the farm, back toward the woods. They all decided that it would be best to stay out of sight of the road as much as possible since Lochlan was the only one of them not wanted by the authorities. He actually was amused by that fact. How a man who'd spent the whole of his life avoiding such complications had landed neck deep in them still mystified him.

It was more like something that would happen to one of his brothers.

They rode for several hours before Bracken took them out of the woods and into the main thoroughfare.

"There's a crossroads up ahead," he explained. "There's oft peddlers and such waiting there for travelers they can sell their wares to. Hopefully someone will be willing to sell us a horse."

Lochlan hoped so. "What about guards?"

"There's a good chance there could be one or two." Bracken narrowed his gaze on the women. "I think we should leave them with Bryce and the two of us ride in."

Lochlan wasn't so sure. "It seems anytime I leave Catarina alone she finds trouble."

She gave him an indignant glare. "I do not . . ." Then her face softened as if she rethought her words. ". . . often."

Lochlan laughed, grateful she could at least acknowledge the truth.

"I'll watch her carefully," Bryce said with a wry twist to his lips. "And if she makes any trouble, I'll tackle her to the ground and tie her down."

Now it was his turn to receive Catarina's scathing glare. "You little scamp. I'll remember that."

He beamed.

Lochlan reined his horse while Bryce took the women away from the road, into hiding. Once he was sure no one could see them, he led Bracken the short distance to the peddlers.

As predicted, there were three carts of vendors with various wares. Lochlan paused at the first one they reached. The man's cart had items of metalwork, including a selection of small swords. Those could come in handy.

After dismounting, he picked up one of the swords to test the blade and balance. It was crudely made, more akin to the ones used by a foot soldier. Hardly fit for a noble knight, but it was the best they would be able to manage until they reached the fair.

Lochlan paid the man, then moved to the next vendor.

Bracken held the horses as Lochlan handed the blade to him. "Thank you."

"I'll provide you with better in Rouen."

"Trust me, this is the finest blade in all the kingdom."

Lochlan understood what he meant. When something was taken from you, the return of any facsimile of it was welcomed.

"Would you like a pretty bit of cloth for you lady-love?" an old crone called from her cart. "We've got some of the finest weave to be found, my lord. Come and see."

Lochlan gave her a charming grin. "'Tis a horse we need, goodwife."

"A horse says you?" A man came out from behind the cart. "Well now, I've just come into one from the last man who bargained with me. What have you to exchange for it?"

"Coin . . . if the beast be worth it."

The man motioned for him to step behind the cart, where there were three horses tied. The largest was a bay with a white star on its forehead. "It's a gelding," the man explained. "A bit under-nourished, but healthy nonetheless."

Lochlan exchanged a suspicious look with Bracken. The man was right, the horse needed a good meal in its belly, but other than that, it appeared stout. "What do you think?"

Bracken shrugged. "Beggars can't be choosers."

That was true enough. Lochlan pulled his purse out to pay the man. As he took the reins of his new acquisition, he noticed Bracken stepping back into the shadows as horses approached.

The vendor cast a furtive look to the nobleman who was riding toward them. He was a stout fellow who was at least five and twoscore years in age. It was obvious from the vendor's reaction that he'd had a run-in or two with the man and didn't care for him.

"Good day, my lord," the vendor greeted, but the nobleman merely sneered at the vendor and continued on his way.

"Thank God he didn't stop," the old woman said under her breath. "He took all our profits last week for taxes, he said. But I notice he's wearing new boots and a fur tunic while we're eating rotten cabbage."

Lochlan didn't move until after the man and his escorts had ridden past without so much as glancing in their direction. As soon as he was gone, Bracken took the horse and started back toward the others.

"A friend?" Lochlan asked.

"More like . . . a well-deserved customer."

Lochlan grinned. "Last week's supper?"

"Two nights back, actually. Recent enough that I'm quite sure he remembers my face."

"Am I asking for trouble by taking you to Rouen?"

"Most likely."

Lochlan shook his head. Prudence would dictate he leave Bracken and his family to their own means, but he wasn't that type of man. Bracken needed his life back and that would never happen should the man be hanged for crimes he was forced to commit.

"We'd best keep to the woods."

"I couldn't agree more. You never know when more of my clients might be lurking to snare me." There was no mistaking the gleeful light in his eyes.

"You're enjoying this way too much."

"While bitterness can take the joy out of many things, it will also give you a sense of facetious humor. Since it's the source of most amusement these days, I tend to savor these moments."

Lochlan supposed he couldn't blame him. He'd always been one to take humor wherever he could find it himself and he noticed that Bracken handed Lochlan's small purse of coins to the vendor.

Once they were finished, they found the women

and Bryce sitting on the ground, playing a game of dice, waiting for them. Lochlan paused at the sight. He couldn't imagine a lady, never mind a princess, so comfortable with herself that she would deign to sit on the ground to play a common game. Yet there they were and they appeared as happy as they could be.

Bracken gave Catarina a slight bow. "Your mount awaits you, my lady."

Catarina smiled as she pushed herself up to inspect the horse. "And a fine mount he is." She patted the horse's head before rubbing its neck. The beast seemed completely content to be the source of her affection. Not that Lochlan blamed the horse. He'd love to have that particular woman stroke him a bit, too.

Lochlan pulled the feed sack from his saddlebags. "We should probably let him eat a bit before we start."

Bracken agreed. "Aye, he won't be doing us any good if he collapses from hunger."

"And it most certainly would ruin my day as well," Catarina said playfully. "I've no desire to kill a poor, defenseless animal, especially not one so beautiful."

The horse preened as if it understood her.

Once it had eaten, they mounted and returned

to their journey. Lochlan didn't say much as Bryce and Julia teased one another and Catarina, who took their words in stride.

Their comradery made him miss his own brothers greatly. He hadn't realized just how lonely he'd been on this trip until now. He'd spent weeks conversing with no one. Only himself for company—not that he'd minded, but this was infinitely better than talking to his horse.

"So tell us about Scotland, Lord Lochlan," Julia said, pulling his thoughts to her. "I've heard 'tis a wild place where the men barely dress as humans."

Catarina laughed. "Obviously the men dress as human. Look at Lochlan. He's not . . . well too strange."

He smiled. "Compared to what? From what I've seen of the likes of you, we Scots are the best dressed and mannered of the bunch." He looked to Julia. "It's God's country, lass. You've never seen anything more beautiful. The hills and mountains rise up like the backs of giants reaching toward the clearest skies you'll ever see."

"I can't wait to see it."

Catarina gave a low laugh. "You know I can almost taste the heather when you talk about Scotland."

"I wouldn't advise tasting it though," Lochlan teased. "Your luck, you'd be poisoned by it."

"Good point."

They traveled through the day and didn't stop until dusk. Lochlan went hunting for food while the others made camp for the night. It didn't take long to find two hares. He strung them up and made his way back.

As he neared the stream by their camp so that he could wash up, he heard Catarina say his name.

"Lochlan is a bit stern."

He knew he shouldn't be eavesdropping, but at the same time, the women shouldn't have been discussing him either. Deciding that two wrongs might make a right, he crept closer to see the two women at the edge of the water, washing their faces.

"He seems very withdrawn," Julia said. "Like there's something inside him that's hurting."

"He's worried over his missing brother and family, I think."

"Perhaps, but I heard stories about his father. They say the MacAllister was insane. Do you think he might have passed that on to his son?"

"Nay." The sincerity in Catarina's face touched him. "Lochlan's a good man. Look at how he offered all of you a home."

"I know. 'Twas more than fair and decent of him. It's just . . ." Her voice trailed off.

"What?"

Julia swallowed before she continued. "I heard that when the MacAllister was in England at court, they found a girl, ten-and-eight—my age, who'd been raped and beaten to death. The last person who'd seen her said that she'd been going to meet the MacAllister for a tryst. There were many who said he'd killed her during it."

"But they didn't arrest him?"

"Nay they did not. Still . . . what if he had? Do you think Lord Loch—"

"Nay, child," Catarina snapped. "Never. It's not in him to do such a thing."

Lochlan moved back, away from them as their words haunted him. Most likely his father had done it. He wouldn't be surprised.

The only thing people respect is cruelty. Show them you're the meanest and none will dare to attack you. His father had lived and died by those words. And his own mother had worn enough bruises that Lochlan knew firsthand how seldom his father had spared his fist.

Not to mention the rest of them.

But at least Catarina had seen the truth. He was not his father. He refused to deal such cruelty to others. Unfortunately, many others didn't see things the same way Catarina did.

His heart heavy, he returned to camp.

Bryce's face lightened the instant he saw the hares. "There will be full bellies tonight."

Lochlan laid them out by the boy's feet so that he could skin them. "I should wash up." And this time when he made his way back to the stream, he made sure to make enough noise to warn the women of his approach.

Julia quickly excused herself while Catarina stayed behind. Ignoring her, Lochlan knelt to wash his hands.

Cat frowned. Lochlan seemed even more closed off from her than he'd been before. "Are you all right?"

"I'm fine, lass."

But he didn't seem fine. There was something troubling him. "Are we slowing you down?"

"What?"

"I was wondering if you were bothered by the fact that all of us are traveling with you now. I know you're in a hurry to find out about your brother."

"Nay. Since Bracken knows where he's heading and I don't, I imagine this is much quicker."

She moved closer to him. "Then what's weighing on your mind?"

He stood up to tower over her. "There's nothing."

As if she believed him. Every part of his tense body and his pale eyes denied his claim. "If you say so, my lord."

He frowned at her. "What do you mean by that tone of voice?"

"Nothing at all. If your mind is empty, then it's empty. Far be it from me to question a mindless man."

His scowl deepened. "I thought you said you would refrain from insulting me."

"It appears I can't help myself. Must be your charming ways that compel me to tease you so. Besides, you told Bracken that what with your brothers, you were used to being insulted."

His features smoothed a bit. "I was rather enjoying the hiatus from my torment."

"Then I shall give you peace once more." Cat moved away from him, but before she could take more than one step, he gently took her arm.

She looked up expectantly as a myriad of emotions crossed his brow. But the one that made her ache was the torment she saw in those pale eyes. He wanted to say something, she could feel. However, he seemed incapable of getting it out.

"Is there something more?"

He let go. "Nay. You should return." He knelt back on the ground.

Cat hesitated as she watched him splash water on his face. Part of her wanted to go to him and touch his rigid back. But the other could sense he wanted to be alone. Deciding to give him peace, she forced herself to walk away even though it was hard.

She didn't know why she wanted to soothe him, yet she did. There was something about him that lured her even against common sense. She'd never felt like this about a man before. Sure, there had been men like Bracken who appealed to her in terms of looks and personality. Men who made her laugh and who were extremely attractive. But they didn't make her warm just to glance at them. She didn't want to soothe them when they were sad; nor did she ache simply because she thought they were troubled.

"Are you all right?" Bracken asked, as she returned to camp.

Suddenly she understood Lochlan's reticence to answer. "I'm fine."

"You don't look fine."

"Of course I do. At least as fine as someone running from the authorities. All in all, I think I appear quite happy."

He laughed. "I've always admired that about you."

"What?"

"Your ability to make light of any situation, no matter how dire. It's a skill I wish I possessed."

Cat smiled at him. "You are too kind. I think all of you have immense grace under pressure." She moved past him to see Julia and Bryce fastening a makeshift spit above the fire so that they could cook the hares.

Once it was complete and they had the hares dressed and roasting, Bryce pulled out a small wooden flute from his satchel and began to play.

Closing her eyes, she listened to the notes and let the pleasure of them ease the worry in her mind. She didn't know why, but the sound of music had always soothed her no matter what. She opened her eyes and smiled at the young man. "You've grown very talented."

He paused in his song to smile at her. "Thanks, Cat." Then he returned to playing.

Cat held her hand out to Julia. "Dance with me, Jules."

She got up without hesitation and brushed the dirt from her skirt. Laughing, she took Cat's hands so that they could turn a circle together.

* * *

Lochlan paused as he entered camp as saw the women dancing together. But what froze him to the spot was the way Cat danced. It wasn't anything like he'd seen before. Unlike the dancers at court, she undulated and moved like a seductress. If this was how Salome had looked, he could well understand a man willing to do anything to placate such a woman.

The sound of her laughter and song caressed his ears. And when she spun alone the hem of her dress lifted, showing him the most incredible set of legs he'd ever beheld.

Catarina danced without care. Without rules. All that mattered to her was her enjoyment.

Her smile floored him as she came to his side and held her hands out to him. "Join us, Lochlan."

Never in his life had he wanted anything more, but he couldn't. He didn't know how and the last thing he wanted was to look foolish before the others. "Nay, thank you."

She tsked at him. "Come, my lord. For one moment, be free."

He glanced to Bracken, who watched them curiously. "Nay, Catarina."

Rolling her eyes at him, she went to Bracken,

who took up her invitation with the same abandon.

A part of him hated the man in that instant. But the truth was he hated himself most of all. He could just as easily have danced, too. Only he was stopping himself.

You'll look like a fool, boy. Men don't dance. Only women, geldings, and jesters. If you want a woman to mock you, have at it. Trust me, they only care how a man battles on the field and how he performs in their bed.

His father was right. Besides, the one time he'd danced, the woman he'd loved had gone to bed with someone else . . .

Lochlan flinched at the harsh reminder. To please Maire, he'd belittled himself and it hadn't been enough. He would never again stoop to such a level. People could take him as he was and if he wasn't good enough for them, then he was better off without them.

So he contented himself with watching the others dance.

Until he realized the hares were burning.

Cursing, he ran to the spit to turn it, but it was too late. One side was already blackened.

Breathless, Catarina joined. "Oh no!"

"You see what such foolery gets you, don't you?" he snapped.

She didn't even react to it other than to laugh. "Aye, blackened hare and a smile. I'll take that over morbidity any day."

He wanted to argue, but the twinkle in her eye won him over and he returned her smile.

"One day, Lochlan, I will have you dance."

"That will never happen, lass."

"Are you challenging me?"

"Nay, I only speak the truth."

Still her eyes were merry. "As do I and I will have my way with you. Mark my words."

The only problem was at this moment, he wanted to have his own way with her in an entirely differ-ent kind of dance. He could feel the heat from her body and was desperate to taste her lips, among other parts of her.

"You'd best let me take that," Julia said as she jostled him aside and took over roasting the hares. "We can't afford for any more of the hares to burn; otherwise, you'll have to be hunting again."

He nodded even though he wasn't quite sure what the girl said. He was too fixated on Catari-na's mouth.

Her dark eyes glistened mischievously before

she stood up on her tiptoes and placed a quick kiss to his cheek. "One dance," she whispered in his ear.

Chills spread over him, but they were quickly squelched by the knowledge that he would never yield to her charms.

And he would never dance.

Chapter 7

Even though they were all a bit nervous about the ones chasing them, the road to Rouen was uneventful. Not that their stress was alleviated by their arrival at the fair. Here there were king's men all over, some of whom could easily identity Bracken or Cat.

She only hoped none of them knew that her father was currently seeking her.

Julia's face brightened at the sight of the multicolored tents and competing music that surrounded them. It'd been a while since Cat had been to a fair this large. There were people all around them. Spectators, entertainers, and knights rushing to and from. There was a liveliness here that made her spirits soar.

"Jugglers!" Julia said, twisting in her saddle to watch them as they rode past. "Now there's a talent I'd dearly love to have."

Bryce scoffed at his sister's interest. "Think you the jousts are still going on?" he asked Lochlan.

"Most likely," Lochlan said. "They usually run to the very end."

"I can't wait until I'm old enough to compete."

Bracken scoffed. "Spoken like a boy who has yet to be knocked off a horse, onto his backside. I think you'll change your mind once you've tasted a piece of lance."

"It never stopped you."

Julia smirked. "That's because he took such a blow to his head in his first match that it addled his brains and they haven't worked properly since."

"Ow!" Bracken snapped. "I'm being attacked by both of you snipes at once. Where is chivalry?"

"Certainly not here, Lord Grump," Julia said an instant before she set her heels to her horse and rode on ahead of them.

Bryce frowned. "Does she know where we're going?"

"I would say not."

The boy let out a sound of disgust before he went after her.

"Where are we headed?" Bracken asked.

Lochlan reined his horse before he handed his money to Bracken. "You find us tents to rent and I'll see about finding this Stryder." He dismounted and handed his reins to Bracken. "I'll catch up to you later."

Bracken inclined his head to him.

Before Lochlan could take so much as a single step, Cat slid from her horse and joined him. "I'll come, too."

He wasn't so sure that was the wisest course of action. "You'd do better to stay with Bracken."

"Nay. I would rather help you search."

Lochlan started to argue, but he knew better. There was never winning a verbal argument with this woman. Unwilling to waste time or breath, he headed for the nearest gathering of nobles.

They paused their discussion at his approach.

"Forgive my intrusion. I'm trying to locate Stryder of Blackmoor."

Two of the men burst out laughing while the others appeared less than amused.

Lochlan exchanged a confused look with Catarina before the one of the laughing men sobered.

He cleared his throat. "Stryder is on the field.

If you want to speak to him, you'd better don armor. He's not exactly in a friendly mood."

His words brought more laughter from the others.

"Is there something I should know about the man?"

"Aye, he's been fighting with his wife all week. She's holed up in the castle while he stands in the list. He's in the foulest of moods, so unless you come bearing a peace offering with Rowena, I doubt he'll be interested in anything you have to say."

That wasn't something he wanted to hear. Damn. The last thing he needed to do was walk into the midst of a marital spat.

Catarina pulled him away from the men. "I have an idea."

Before he could ask after it, she headed for the castle. "Catarina?"

"Trust me, Lochlan."

Did he have a choice? She was quickly making her way through the crowd, oblivious to everyone around her. What the devil was she about?

In fact, she didn't pause until she was inside the hall, where a small group had gathered. Lochlan hesitated as he heard laughter and music.

Catarina approached a guard to their right. "Beg

pardon, sir. Can you tell me where I might find the Countess of Blackmoor?"

The man smiled down at her. "Hear that voice that sounds like an angel in heaven? That be she, milady. She's in the hall singing."

"Thank you."

Lochlan finally understood what Catarina was about. What better way to tame the lion and bring him to heel than to win over his lioness? It made sense to seek the lady out first and since Catarina was also a woman, no one would think it untoward of them.

Catarina headed for the small gathering of nobles. Lochlan stood back, afraid of disturbing them. Or worse, fearing one of them might wish to cause more angst between Rowena and Stryder and report to the earl that Lochlan had been seen speaking to his wife.

But luckily the countess was all but finished. She sang the last note and then handed her lute over to a young man to her left. He had to give Stryder credit, the countess was as beautiful as she was talented. With long blond hair and bright eyes, she was definitely striking.

The crowd applauded and cheered for her. She took her bow, then started away from them.

"Countess?" Catarina called.

She paused. "Aye? Do I know you?"

"Nay. I've come here with a friend." Catarina glanced back at him and motioned him to move closer. "We must needs speak with your husband."

The countess's eyes sharpened as anger darkened her cheeks. "Then I suggest you don armor and seek him on the field as that is the only place that man cares to be." She started away from them.

"Please," Catarina said. "'Tis of dire importance. Lord Lochlan is seeking information on his brother who vanished in the Holy Land. He was told Lord Stryder was the last to see him alive."

Those words succeeded in making the countess stop. "Outremer?"

Lochlan nodded. "We thought Kieran was dead. But a man bearing his plaid was killed in Scotland. I was told Lysander once—"

"Lysander," she breathed. The anger fled her face. "Exceptionally tall and dark-haired?"

"Aye."

Cat froze as she realized something. The countess was very concerned and if her husband had once been a captive in Outremer like Lysander . . .

She lowered her voice so that no one could overhear them. "Is Lord Stryder a member of the Brotherhood of the Sword?"

Rowena cast her gaze about furtively. "How do you know the Brotherhood?"

"Lysander and Pagan were like family to me. I traveled with them."

Recognition lit the countess's eyes. "Are you Cat?"

"Aye."

All the suspicion left her face and was replaced by instant friendship. "I've heard many stories about you. 'Tis a pleasure to meet you finally."

"Thank you." She held her hand out toward Lochlan. "This is Lochlan MacAllister, laird of the clan."

And again her face lightened as she heard his name. "You would be Lord Sin's brother?"

"Aye."

"Then we're all practically family, eh?" Rowena grimaced as if she'd had a sudden thought. "But this means I must go make amends with the devil. Plague on the man and all his principles. Fine. 'Tis for a greater good. I do this for another and so the Lord in all his mercy will bless me." She let out a frustrated breath. "At least He'd best bless me. Heaven knows the last thing I want to do is cater to the devil's ego. I've had my fill of it."

Cat glanced to Lochlan, who appeared as baffled as she was. "The devil?"

"My warring husband of course. Now come before I regain my senses and leave you on your own."

Cat laughed at the woman. She didn't know why, but she really liked her. "Thank you, Countess."

"Call me Rowena." She started for the door, looking very much like someone about to call for Last Rites.

Lochlan trailed after the women, trying not to get his hopes up. It was possible that Stryder knew nothing of Kieran's whereabouts. But what if he did? What if, by some miracle, Stryder had seen him recently?

It was hard to keep himself in check. This was the closest he'd been . . . At last, he might have an answer to his brother's fate.

Rowena led them straight to the tourney field. Without stopping, she went to the tent that was set up just on the edge of the lists. It was solid black and guarded by a well-muscled man who snapped to attention as he saw Rowena's approach.

She inclined her head to him. "Good day, Val. Is the boor inside?"

"More like a boar with a raging tusk, my lady, if you take my meaning. Please have mercy on us all and speak with him."

"Unfortunately, I must. But I promise you, it won't improve his mood if I can help it."

The man looked pained. "Thanks, my lady. Your kindness knows no boundaries."

"And I'll remember that tone when next you beg favor from me."

"I am quite sure you will."

"Counsel your tongue when you address my wife." The surly growl coming out of the tent sounded like thunder. "That is your lady you speak to. You'd do well to remember it."

Rowena looked less than pleased. "Don't think taking up for me is going to get you back in my good graces, Warmonger."

Stryder left the tent like an emerging dragon. His long, dark, wavy hair hung just past his shoulders. And even though he was angry, he had kind and intelligent eyes. "Think you by now I don't know that? You'll not be placated until I make an arse of myself before the entire court. I've done that once and . . ." His voice trailed off as he realized they weren't alone.

"Ha!" Rowena said triumphantly. "Look, you've

already made a fool of yourself. What's a little more humiliation?"

Stryder grimaced at his wife.

Cat suppressed her smile as she took a step forward. "Please forgive us our interruption, my lord. But Lord Lochlan would like a word with you in private."

Stryder glared at his wife before he started away. "I haven't time for this."

Arms akimbo, Rowena put herself in his path. "You can run innocent men through with your lance later." She picked up his gauntleted hand and held it in hers. "He has important"—she squeezed his hand tight—"business indeed."

Understanding lightened the earl's eyes. "Please join me in my tent."

Lochlan allowed the women to go first before he followed the earl inside. The tent was surprisingly large, with a nice-sized bed and table set up. Stryder indicated the women to sit down before he faced Lochlan.

"Are you from Outremer?" Stryder asked him.

"Nay. I was told my brother knew you there."

Stryder scowled. "Your brother?"

"Kieran MacAllister."

The was no mistaking the pain that flared deep in the man's blue eyes. Rowena actually stood up and moved to his side. She didn't say a word, but she patted his back affectionately and it was obvious the man took strength from her touch.

"You must be his brother Lochlan. He said all his brothers were dark-haired save you."

Emotions flooded him at those words. It was true. Stryder had known his brother and Kieran hadn't died in the loch after all. He could almost cry in relief, but that wasn't in him. "Aye. I'm Lochlan."

Stryder squeezed his wife before he left her to walk over to a trunk by his bed. "Kieran was a good man."

Lochlan couldn't breathe as fear assailed him. "Was?"

He nodded. "Outremer changed many of us. Not necessarily for the better. There were two Scots among our prisoners. Brothers they said. MacAllisters."

It couldn't be. "Two?" How was that possible?

"Aye. Kieran and Duncan." He pulled a small box from the trunk and returned to Lochlan's side. He handed it over. "Kieran gave me that two days before we escaped. He told me to hold on to it in the event one of his brothers should ever look for him. It was his hope that all of you would continue to think him dead—he didn't want you to know what had become of him. But his fear would be that one of you would learn the truth, then seek him out."

His hand shaking, Lochlan opened the box and felt tears sting his eyes. It was a small silver crucifix identical to the one he carried. The crosses had been gifts from their mother as each one reached his maturity. And just like his, it bore Kieran's name engraved on the back of it.

"Kieran said you would recognize it and know that it was his."

"I do." Swallowing, he met Stryder's gaze. "Is my brother . . ." He couldn't bring himself to say the words. The fear of the answer choked him and he couldn't bear the thought of knowing his brother had died in the Holy Land and none of them had known it.

"Alive?" Stryder finished, "I don't know. The MacAllister brothers stayed behind and fought the Saracens while we escaped . . . one died that night and the other . . ." He flinched from the memory.

"What of him?"

"He lives in England now. Silent and hidden."

"Is it Kieran?" Lochlan's voice cracked.

"I honestly don't know. The two men looked so much alike they could have been twins. There were many times during our imprisonment that we weren't sure which one was Duncan and which one was Kieran."

"But you have to know if it's him. Surely."

"The Scot is severely disfigured," Rowena breathed. "He would have died had his brother not saved him and Stryder not carried him to Europe. The fighting claimed one life and the other . . . we can't tell who he is and he won't say."

Stryder nodded. "He went into seclusion and has never emerged."

Lochlan stood there completely stunned by the unexpected turn. He wanted to laugh and curse.

Catarina wrapped her arms around his. "We can go and see if it's Kieran."

"Aye." He looked back at Stryder. "Where is he?"

"He's in a remote keep in Sussex. If you can wait a few days, I can take you there. It's the only way he'll allow you to approach. The Scot trusts no one. The last man who tried to broach his lands was shot four times."

Cat gaped. "Did he die?"

"Nay, but I assure you no one else has tried to visit since without a member of the Brotherhood at his side."

Strangely enough, that sounded just like something the hotheaded Kieran would do. Lochlan held his hand out to Stryder. "I can't tell you how much I appreciate this."

He shook his arm and patted him on the shoulder. "Have no fear. I have a brother myself and there's nothing I wouldn't do for him."

No wonder he was so willing to help. "Is he here?"

"Nay. Ironically, he's with the Scot for the time being, which is another reason I don't mind taking you. It's been almost a year since I last saw Kit." He looked at Rowena. "That is if my wife is agreeable?"

"Aye. For this I will go and will even be willing to speak to you on the journey since it's for a good cause, unlike the unnatural tendency you have to want to knock grown men down with a stick."

Stryder rolled his eyes.

Rowena's gaze softened. "Now be at banquet tonight, husband. Alexander and William miss their father and I grow weary of their complaints." She left before Stryder could respond.

"William and Alexander?" Cat asked.

"Our sons. Since their mother banned me from her chambers in the keep, I haven't been able to see them. Rowena fears they'll become corrupted by my warring ways."

Lochlan was baffled by his words. "Did she not understand you were a knight when she married you?"

"Aye, but her greatest fear is to see me fall in battle as her father did and so she ever nettles me over this. Once the tourney ends and I still live, she will be fine." A small smile toyed at the edges of lips. "I have learned that the rose is worth putting up with a few thorns from time to time. I know it is only her fear that makes her churlish and if she didn't love me so, she wouldn't care what befalls me. So I welcome her rancor at tourney, but please for the love of God, never tell her that. I fear should it ever grow worse."

Lochlan laughed. "Your secret is safe."

"Good, now if you'll excuse me, I need to prepare for my next match."

Lochlan followed Cat outside and waited until they were alone again. "So tell me of this secretive Brotherhood of the Sword."

Cat took a breath as she thought about her friends Pagan and Lysander and the scars, both physical and mental, they'd borne. "They were all prisoners in Outremer. They were held in the same Saracen camp. Stryder was one of the group's leaders and he and the others found a way to escape. But as you heard, the escape didn't go completely smoothly and many never made it home. Those who did set up a network of people to help return others to their families and to help the newly freed to acclimate to their homes again. They are called the Brotherhood of the Sword and they all bear the mark of a crescent moon and scimitar brand on their hands."

Lochlan ground his teeth as he tried to imagine the horrors Kieran must have seen in such a place. He'd heard enough tales of Saracen jails to know that all of them would be scarred severely from it. If the Scot was his brother, he wondered if Kieran were still sane.

"This Pagan you traveled with—"

"He was a good man, but he refused to speak of the prison. Lysander would get drunk and relay events to us. It was truly horrifying." She reached out to touch him. "I'm so sorry that your brother ended up there."

"As am I." If he could, he would gladly have changed places with Kieran.

Catarina took his hand in hers. "What happened that he left?"

"A fight. There was a woman, Isobail, with whom he fell in love. She was supposed to marry someone else and so he ran away with her in the middle of the night, supposedly to save her from her future husband—it was what caused our clans to go to war with one another. Kieran brought her to our home and we welcomed her in. But even from the beginning I knew she was trouble. She even came on to me one night after Kieran had retired."

"Did you tell him?"

"I tried and he laughed at me for it. It wasn't until she turned her attention to our brother Ewan that Kieran realized I was right. As she'd done with Kieran, she talked Ewan into leaving with her in the middle of the night. She had him take her to England, where another lover was waiting. She abandoned Ewan and almost ruined his life. He came home, but by then it was too late. Kieran had vanished. He left his sword and plaid on the shore of a loch not far from our home, so we all assumed he'd drowned himself in grief."

"But he hadn't."

Lochlan winced. "If only I'd known. I should have sought him. But my mother and Ewan were so destroyed that I never even considered the possibility that Kieran would have feigned his own death. What kind of arse would do such a thing?"

"Someone who was hurting so much that he couldn't see past his own pain to someone else's."

Anger roiled through him. "It was selfish."

"Aye. Such things always are. He must have been young."

"He was." Still, it was no excuse to have destroyed their mother with grief.

"Then you should forgive him."

"Could you?"

"I'm not saying I wouldn't beat him for it, but in the end to have him back . . ."

Lochlan nodded. She did understand. There was a relief inside him at the thought of seeing his brother again . . . He would give anything to know his brother was alive.

And he hated the thought of what Catarina's family must be going through not knowing what had befallen her. "We need to get you back to your uncle."

"We will. I have faith that all things happen for a reason and that he will return to my life when God wills it."

Her faith amazed him. She possessed an inner peace that was unfathomable to him. Even though her father was trying to control her life, even when everything around her was in complete chaos, she was calm.

Patting his hand, she smiled up at him. "Do you think the Scot could be Kieran?"

"I'm not sure. Either way it appears I'll have a brother again." The only question seemed to be if it would be the brother he'd grown up with or another he'd never known about. Even if it were Kieran, he'd have to learn him all over again. So much had happened since the day of his disappearance . . .

Lochlan wasn't sure if this was a curse or a blessing. But then again, he had a brother out there. How could that be anything other than a blessing?

No, this was wonderful and he refused to see it as anything else.

It took them a bit of time to find Bracken and his siblings. They'd rented two small tents that were at the back of the field. One for the women and one for the men.

"Did you find Stryder?" Bracken asked.

"Aye. We'll . . ." He paused as he realized that he couldn't take Bracken to England. He'd completely forgotten about the man's banishment. "I'll have to hire a boat to take you into Scotland. Catarina and I shall have to journey back through England to find my brother."

"You're right about that," Bracken concurred.

"My trail through England would be a bloody one indeed. 'Tis that whole nasty banishment problem that gets in the way. And no offense, I'd rather keep my head attached to my body a bit longer."

"I certainly can't blame you for that."

"Bracken?" Julia asked, interrupting them. "Would it be possible now that Lord Lochlan and Cat are back for Bryce and me to tour the activities?"

Bracken hesitated before he gave a hard stare at Bryce. "You are responsible for your sister. No getting distracted and wandering off from her. Do you hear me?"

"I do."

"Then off with you, but I want you both back here before dark. There's all kinds of people here."

"Some of whom could be thieves," Cat teased.

"Aye, and no picking purses or pockets. We're honest now and I expect you both to behave like the nobles you are."

Julia lifted her chin indignantly. "I'm offended to the marrow of my bones that you would think I would stoop so low." She swept her gaze first to Bryce, then to Bracken. "You two were the thieves.

Even dressed as a boy, I was always a lady." And with that, she left in a snit.

Bracken let out an angry growl. "Bryce, keep an eye on her and if any man so much as glances her way, you have my permission to gut him. And if anything untoward happens to Julia, then I will gut you."

Bryce all but ran out of the tent.

Bracken turned toward Lochlan. "Be glad you have brothers. Nothing worse than having a sister who is entirely too attractive for your mental health."

Cat laughed. "Now Bracken, Julia has a fine head on her shoulders. She's not the type to fall for a man's beauty or let him sway her. I assure you, she'd never do anything to shame you or herself."

"I know. It's the men I don't trust. We're all lying, deceitful dogs when it comes to chasing after a pretty girl."

Lochlan stiffened. "I'm offended by that. I've never lied to a woman."

"That's why God must have given you brothers. I assure you, when it comes to Julia, I'm paying well for my past sins."

Lochlan laughed. "Then come. Let us find armor

and a good sword for you while we're here . . . just in case you should need one."

Cat shook her head. "All the better to gut, eh?"

Bracken pulled his sword from his belt and ran his thumb down the blade. "You know, the duller and cruder the blade, the more the gutting would hurt . . ."

"Then you can save that sword for Julia's suitors."

"Aye, I think I will." He sheathed it at his side.

Without thinking, Cat followed the men out of the tent, into the crowd. They'd only taken a few steps when a bad feeling went through her.

It wasn't until a man wearing a silver mask paused beside her that she understood why.

"Good day, Cousin Catarina."

Chapter 8

Cat couldn't breathe as she realized the man in the mask was Damien St. Cyr. His mother was the sister of Cat's father and it'd been years since she last saw him. In those days, he'd been a beautiful but arrogant boy, always boasting about his lineage and the lands he'd one day inherit. Cat had never cared for him.

But the man in front of her seemed different from the boy she'd known and it wasn't just the fact that he had an ornate silver mask covering the upper part of his face. There was air of powerful restraint and it wasn't just from the fact that he was tall and well built.

He was awe-inspiring and mysterious.

"Cousin Damien," she said, hating the note of panic she heard in her voice. The boy she'd known wouldn't have hesitated to sic her father or his men on her. He'd even relish it and whatever pain they'd put her through. "I didn't expect to find you here." But she should have. It would only have made sense that some of her large French family would be at a fair this size.

Shame on her for not considering that more carefully.

"I should say the same of you." He leaned down so that only she could hear his next words. "Especially since all of France is looking for you."

Her stomach shrank.

"Don't worry," he whispered, touching her cheek lightly with his gloved hand. "Your secret is safe with me." He straightened and snapped his fingers. "Henri, donate your cloak to my dearest cousin. I fear she might be a bit chilled."

Without hesitation, the man behind him whipped his cloak off and handed it to Damien, who then wrapped it around her. He raised the cowl to hide her face and offered her a genuine smile as he tucked her hair in.

"There are three besides me who will know you.

Stay out of the great hall and away from the tourney field and you should be fine."

She still couldn't believe he was doing this for her. It had never been in his nature to help anyone. "Why are you helping me?"

There was a flash of pain in his eyes that he quickly shielded. "Let's just say, I know what it's like to be held against my will. It's something I would wish on no one." And with that, he left her.

Cat gaped as he led his entourage away. Luckily, none of them even looked back at her. She crossed herself in relief.

"Catarina? Is anything amiss?"

She started at Lochlan's voice as he returned to her side with a worried frown. "Nay. I just met my cousin."

Panic flashed across his brow.

"He let me go." She was still incredulous. "I can't believe he'd be so kind."

Lochlan glanced around as if looking for him. "Neither can I. Are you sure he won't call out the guards once he finds them?"

If he'd asked her that question before this meeting, she would have said aye. It would have been just the sort of thing the boy Damien would have done. Now, she wasn't so sure.

"Nay, I think we're safe."

And she did, too.

Bracken walked back toward them. "Is something wrong? I looked behind me and both of you had disappeared."

Lochlan indicated her with a jerk of his chin. "Catarina met her cousin here a few moments ago."

His eyes widened in surprise. "Which one?"

Cat couldn't wait to see what his next expression would be since he thought even less of the man than she did. "Damien St. Cyr."

Bracken reached for his hilt as he scanned the crowd with a feral grimace. "Is the bastard calling out guards?"

"Nay," she said breathlessly. "He gave me this cloak to hide with and told me to be careful lest they find me."

This time, Bracken's jaw dropped. "Damien . . . St. Cyr told you that? Damien-I-have-no-soul-St.-Cyr? Satan's misbegotten demonspawn? The same demented boy who cut the strap on my saddle the first time I jousted and laughed when I broke my leg and collarbone?"

Actually, she'd forgotten about that one misdeed—there had been so many such events in their childhoods. "Aye. The same."

Bracken snorted. "What the hell happened to him that he'd find decency now?"

She shrugged, every bit as baffled by it as he was. "Maybe he just grew up?"

Still, there was doubt in Bracken's eyes. "More like he took a stiff blow to his head. Trust me, 'twould take much more than that for the devil to change his ways. He used to live to hurt others."

Now Lochlan was looking sheepish.

Cat patted Bracken's arm. "You're right, but I think he's different now."

"Then get the name of whatever priest exorcised him. We need to send the man a gift of appreciation."

"Bracken," she chided. "Have more charity. And let us be glad that he's on our side in this." The one thing no one ever wanted was to have Damien against them. As Bracken had said, the man could be pure evil.

Bracken scoffed as he renewed his quest through the crowd. "I'm still not sure he's not off to tell others where you are. They could be planning to take you even as we speak. Most likely at a time when you least expect it."

She shook her head. "Well that's something I don't wish to think of."

While they argued, Lochlan paused as they

reached an armorer's stand. He held up a long sword to test it.

Looking pleased with the weapon, he passed it over to Bracken. "What say you to this?"

Bracken placed his forefinger below the cross hilt to check the balance. "Good proportions and balance. Fine lines."

"You'll not find a better swordmaker in all of Christendom," a youth said as he came out of the tent that was set off to the side of the table. "My father takes great pride in his work."

"And it shows," Cat said, while Bracken swung the sword around his body. "'Tis a most beautiful weapon."

The boy beamed.

Cat stood back while Lochlan outfitted Bracken with everything he would need to fight. She'd never seen Bracken so pleased. There was a light in his eyes now that had been missing before and he stood taller. It was his dignity she realized. With the loss of his father and lands, the man had suffered a harsh blow to his ego. But now he appeared the same nobleman she'd grown to know all those years ago.

It made her happy to see the return of her old friend and she was grateful to Lochlan for giving this to him. It was truly a good deed.

As soon as he was outfitted, Bracken excused himself to go partake of the armed games. But knowing him, she was sure he was off to take revenge on a few nobles and "conquer" them. Cat bit back her smile as he literally ran like a child to join the other men in the list.

She walked up to Lochlan, who was paying the armorer. "That was a noble thing you did just now."

He shrugged his charitable deed aside. "I like to help people, especially those who've had a hard time of it."

Her heart softened. "My mother was like you. I once saw her pull the cloak off her own shoulders to wrap it around an old woman in one of the towns we were passing through. It was freezing cold, but my mother said better it go to the one who needs it most. She was a kind lady."

"And you, lass?"

"I, too. It's how Lysander and Pagan ended up traveling with us. We found them on the road, starving. I invited them to dinner and the next thing my uncle knew, they were permanent fixtures. I would have had it no other way. Bavel used to chide me constantly about picking up strays. He said that one day they would turn on me."

"And did they?"

"Aye. A few. And it was one such stray who kidnapped me from my uncle and tried to deliver me to my father. I still can't believe he betrayed me after all we did for him."

Lochlan turned toward her as the armorer left them to wait on another customer. "I'm sorry, Catarina."

She sighed before she stepped away. "Don't be. I'm the one who has to deal with my father at some point. It merely irks me that he must move through others rather than dealing with me forthright. I am his daughter, yet we are awkward with one another. No child should feel that way around its parent."

She glanced at him as they walked back toward the trail that ran between the tents. His hair was tousled from the wind and his eyes vibrant. "You've no idea how much I hate being my father's bargaining tool."

"I think I have a good idea on that, lass."

Perhaps he did. There was something in his tone that spoke to the pain inside her. "Tell me something, Lochlan? Have you ever used someone this way?"

"Nay. I have not."

"And if you had a daughter—"

"I would treasure her with every part of me."

How she wanted to believe that. "Would you make her marry for the sake of your clan?"

Lochlan paused as he considered it. She gave him credit for the thought and she wondered what he'd say.

"Nay," he spoke at last. "I would never intentionally hurt my child. I'd find another way for peace. One that could make both of us happy."

Cat took his strong hand into hers as those words made her ache. If only her father felt that way.

But it also made her think of Lochlan's betrothed, who waited for him in Scotland. "And how does your future bride feel about marrying you?"

He shrugged. "I know not. However, there is nothing settled between us yet, so she is not truly my betrothed. I have yet to answer her father's offer."

She cocked her head. Given what he'd said earlier, she couldn't imagine why he would wait. "Why not?"

"Because I don't want a wife who isn't suited to me."

She frowned. "What does that mean?"

He let go of her hand before he started forward. "I need a wife at my side who will be steadfast and clearheaded. One who is intelligent and calm-spirited. I don't want someone who will cause conflict in my home or with my clan, but rather a wife who can shoulder her burdens without complaint."

Cat cringed at what he described. "You speak of her as if she's a horse. You seek a broodmare perhaps?"

He gave her a hostile glare. "Nay. While I hope the Lord sees fit to give me children, there is never any guarantee of that. In the event we are childless, I need a wife who is an asset to my clan, not a hindrance."

While that made sense, it didn't answer her original question. "But what of you the man, Lochlan? What do *you* seek in a woman?"

Lochlan glanced away from her probing stare as unnamed emotions choked him. He wanted what his brothers had. He wanted a woman who could hold him at night and stand by his side during the day. A woman who would love him and cherish him. One whose very presence made his day brighter.

But he would never find that and he knew it, so there was no need even to think about such things. His place was to care for others, not have them care for him. His needs weren't important. Only those of his family and people.

However, she didn't want to hear that. So he posed the same question to her. "Tell me what you want, Catarina? What kind of man would make your heart fly?"

Her eyes were sad and tinged by the same loneliness he felt so often. "There is no man for me."

"But if there were . . . what would he be like?"

When she didn't answer right away, he gave her a knowing smile. "It's not so easy to answer, now is it?"

A tiny smile teased the corner of her lips. "Point well taken, my lord. And you're right. I don't know who that man might be. But I know it's not the obnoxiously spoiled prince my father would see me marry."

And he could well understand that.

"Lochlan!"

Lochlan turned at the sound of a familiar voice. It wasn't until he saw the tall auburn-haired man that he realized who was calling him. It was his brother Sin's foster brother and friend. "Simon," he said, extending his arm to the man as he joined them.

Simon shook it and clapped him on the back. "Long time since our paths last crossed, my friend. How is everyone?"

"Doing very well, and you?"

Simon looked a bit sheepish. "Aside from the fact my wife is pregnant again and can't get comfortable when she sits and has no compunction about letting me know it and sharing said pain, we're all doing remarkably well."

Lochlan smiled before he realized that he hadn't introduced them. "Lord Simon of Anwyk meet . . . Cat."

Cat arched a brow as Lochlan shortened her name for the first time. It actually made sense. The last thing they needed was to have someone recognize her or hear her name and become suspicious.

She didn't know who Simon was, but he seemed an amiable enough fellow. "Lord Simon, 'tis an honor to meet you."

He gave her a courtly bow. "And you, my lady." He looked back and forth between them expectantly.

"We're friends," she explained.

"I see." But by his tone she could tell he was still trying to figure out their relationship.

Deciding to divert his attention, Cat asked a question of her own. "And how is it the two of you know one another?"

"Simon was the foster brother to my brother Sin and he's Sin's best friend," Lochlan explained.

Simon gave her a charming smile. "Aye. I have the scars to prove it."

She arched a brow at his light tone over such a matter. "Scars?"

Still Simon's eyes twinkled merrily. "Hanging around Sin MacAllister and Stryder of Blackmoor can be quite hazardous to one's health. As I said, I have quite the collection of scars to prove it."

She laughed. "So you're friend to Stryder as well. How interesting. He is the reason we're here."

"Aye," he said laughing, "Stryder is the one who told me Lochlan was here. He said you were seeking news of your brother Kieran."

Lochlan nodded. "Lord Stryder has agreed to see us to the Scot once the tourney ends to see if he is Kieran."

Cat was a bit confused by Simon's ignorance. "If you were so close to Lochlan's brother Sin, how did you not know that Kieran was Sin's brother?"

"Family trees are seldom uncomplicated, my lady. At the time I knew Sin, I knew he was half-Scot, but never once in those days did he mention his family name at all. I knew nothing of the Mac-Allisters really from him until I'd returned from Outremer. Perhaps I should have made the connection then, but I, as everyone, assumed Kieran was dead and the two MacAllisters we knew in prison very seldom spoke to me of other brothers." He indicated Lochlan with a tilt of his head. "Lochlan was the only one they mentioned by name and, unfortunately, that name is rather common in the Highlands. I thought nothing of it until today."

It was sad to think he'd been that close to all of them and had never known. But then that was the way of life at times. "Having known them all so well, can you tell us if the Scot is Kieran Mac-Allister?"

Simon passed a sympathetic look to Lochlan. "I don't know any more than Stryder does. We buried the one brother and brought the other back to England. The one who survived would never speak a name. Then again, he seldom speaks at all. For the longest time we thought him mute from his injuries."

She cringed at the thought of the pain he must have known to be so altered. "What happened to them that night?"

"Honestly we don't know. Again, whatever became of them when they stayed behind was never told. But it must have been horrible indeed. Neither of them was ever the kind of man to shirk from anything. And God and his saints know that

I saw them survive things no man should suffer. I don't even want to contemplate what it was that finally broke the Scot."

She looked at Lochlan, who remained silent, but she knew what he must be thinking. Kieran had indeed shirked from his family. He'd run from them all into a hell unimaginable. It made her want to touch him, but she knew he wouldn't welcome that.

Instead, Lochlan paused as if considering something. "Simon? Could I impose upon you to watch over Cat for a brief time? There's a matter I need to attend to."

"Absolutely."

"My thanks."

Cat scowled at him as he walked away. "Well that was certainly abrupt."

"Were you two fighting?"

"Nay. I thought we were getting along famously . . . especially for us."

Simon shrugged. "Perhaps he had to rush to the privy."

She laughed at his unexpected comment. "Possibly. You were raised around all men, weren't you?"

He joined her laughter. "Aye and my lady wife is ever fond of telling me just how much it shows."

Cat liked this man a great deal even though they'd only just met. "How long have you known Lochlan?" she asked, as they made their way through the crowd again.

"Only a few years, but I've known his brother Sin most of my life." He folded his hands behind his back. "What of you, Lady Cat? How long have you known him?"

"Not too terribly long. My cousin married his brother Ewan and now Lochlan is seeing me back to my uncle."

"That's rather nice of him."

"It is."

They walked for several minutes more while Cat tried to think of some way to broach the topic she truly wanted to discuss.

Simon finally stopped her and gave her a pointed stare. "You know, my lady. You can ask me anything."

"Pardon?"

His gaze was warm and open. "I sense in your silence a need to interrogate me over Lochlan and his family."

"How did you know?"

He shrugged. "I've been around many women who were highly inquisitive about the men I've known. I figure you're no different than the others."

It was true, but . . . "I'm not sure if I should be flattered or offended."

His laughter was low and playfully insidious. "I never openly offend anyone . . . behind their backs is another matter entirely."

She shook her head at his playful tone. "I find it hard to believe you could ever do anything dubious."

A strange look fell over his face as his features instantly sobered. "There is much a person is capable of in the right circumstances."

Cat paused as she caught the underlying threat in his voice. "You're one of the Brotherhood, aren't you?"

He gave only the subtlest of nods.

She felt horrible for him. "I didn't know, Simon, please forgive me."

"There's nothing to forgive. You didn't know and I didn't volunteer the information. Besides, I'm not the subject who fascinates you. That would be Lochlan."

She had to force herself to cringe at the truth. "I wouldn't say Lochlan *fascinates* me."

"If you say so, my lady." But his tone was filled with disbelief. "In that case, I'll pretend that I don't notice the way your voice softens whenever you say his name."

His words horrified her. "It does not . . . does it?"

"Aye."

She felt heat creep over her face. "He is not the kind of man who intrigues me. Truly. At all."

"If you say so, my lady."

"I do say so, but—"

"You still want to know about him."

She nodded even though she wanted to continue her denials. Yet what was the use? Simon could obviously see straight through her.

Simon led her away from the crowd, to a small, secluded bench where they could sit and not be overheard. "I don't know much from Lochlan himself. Most of what I know about him and their family comes from his brother."

"And that is?"

Simon took a deep breath before he answered. "I know Sin would lay down his life for him and there aren't many men Sin feels that way about."

That was good to know. "I heard that their father was rather abusive to others."

Simon gave a bitter laugh. "Aye, you could say that and it wasn't just to strangers. He was a drunkard who seldom spared his fist to any of his family. Lochlan did his best to protect his brothers, but from what I hear there was never anyone around to protect him."

Her heart ached with those words. "He's been responsible for the whole of his life, hasn't he?"

"Aye."

That truly saddened her. She hated to hear of anyone in such a state. While her father hadn't always been kind, her mother and her mother's family had been. She'd had an escape from the pain of her father's court and the moment her mother learned of her treatment, she'd stopped it and kept Cat completely protected. How she wished all children could be so fortunate.

"And there's never been a woman who's captured his heart?" she asked quietly.

"Only one."

She was stunned by that. To hear Lochlan speak, she would never have believed it. He acted as if he had no concept of love. "Did he not ask her to marry him?"

"Aye, he did."

Cat was glad she was sitting. Had they still been walking, she would have most likely fallen from the shock of it. "What happened to her? Why didn't he marry her?"

Simon's eyes snapped with fury for his friend.

"When his father learned of it, he made her his mistress."

She felt the pain of those words like a physical blow. Nay . . . surely it wasn't possible. "He did what?"

"He made her his mistress," he repeated, his tone lethal. "Sin said it was his way of teaching Lochlan that all people had a price and that he could trust no one. That no woman would ever look at him as anything more than the laird of his clan. He would be a trophy to them. Something to claim but never anything to love."

Cat was stunned that anyone would be so cold and stupid. And mean. What had happened to his father that he would think no more of people than that? Think no more of his son?

And what kind of woman would be so foolish as to fall for such a deceitful person? "Why would she, if she was involved with Lochlan, take up with his father?"

Simon laughed bitterly. "You ask me to decipher the mind of a woman I've never met? I can barely fathom my own wife's reasoning most days."

Perhaps there was truth to that. People often did the most bizarre things that never made sense to anyone save them.

"Do you know what happened to her?"

He nodded. "She died giving birth to his father's bastard a year later. Sin said that Lochlan was the only one who attended her burial and that every year on the date of her birth and death, he takes flowers to her grave."

It was just the sort of thing Lochlan would do. But oh the pain it must cost him. Why would his father have hurt him so badly?

Suddenly, she felt like a fool for complaining about her own father to him. By comparison, her father was a saint.

"Did the baby survive?"

"Nay, it was buried in her arms."

Cat winced as she also remembered her earlier conversation with Lochlan when she'd thoughtlessly asked him about what type of woman he'd want for his bride. No wonder he felt as he did. He'd already offered his heart to a woman only to have her serve it back to him in pieces. How could anyone hurt another in such a manner?

But then life seemed to be nothing except pain.

And in that moment of sympathy, she wanted to do something nice for him. But what?

"Tell me, Lord Simon, does Lochlan have something he enjoys doing?"

He looked baffled by her sudden switch of topic. "Such as?"

"Chess? An instrument he plays? Anything of that nature?"

"Nothing Sin ever mentioned and nothing I've ever seen him do."

Cat paused to look about the various vendors who surrounded them. Nothing stood out among their wares that looked like Lochlan. He was a simple man with simple needs.

And then she saw it . . .

There, across the way. A smile curved her lips as she rose from her bench and headed toward the stand. There were several nobles in front of the table, glancing over the wares.

Ignoring them, she picked up the small toy that was carved to look like a monkey. She pressed the bottom and watched as it rocked back and forth. Its tiny mouth opened and closed, making a clicking noise. It was perfect.

Unlike Lochlan, it was completely frivolous. And it was just what such a stern man needed.

"Would milady like for us to wrap her toy?" an older male merchant asked.

Smiling even wider, she handed it to him. "Aye, please."

Simon frowned at her as he joined her and she paid the man for the toy. "Is it a gift for a child?"

"Nay. It's for my protector."

"Lochlan?"

She nodded. "I think he could use a bit of merriment. He seems far too somber to me."

Simon scratched at cheek as he looked skeptical. "I'm not sure how he'll welcome this gift."

Neither was she. "I suppose we'll find out, eh?"

"I suppose."

She thanked the merchant as he returned with her parcel. Taking it from him, she started back toward their tent.

Lochlan paused in the crowd as he again had the feeling that he was being watched. He scanned the people around him, but he couldn't find anyone who seemed to be the least bit interested in him. Still the feeling was there, tingling his skin and begging him to look until he found the source of it.

"Lochlan?"

He turned to see Julia heading for him, with Bryce three steps behind. "Aye, lass?"

"Would you please escort me about so that Bryce may be free to annoy someone else? The saints as my witness if I don't have peace from him soon, I shall have to kill him."

Lochlan suppressed a smile at her mortal tone.

Bryce let out a disgusted breath. "I have no choice. Bracken will kill me if I don't. Think you I enjoy watching you fawn over stupid woman things? Oooh, aah," he mocked in falsetto. "How lovely. How beautiful. This would make a most splendid gown . . . It's only cloth for Peter's sake. Who cares what it feels like?"

She growled at her brother. "You're such a boy."

"And glad of it. Especially if it'll save me from the need to pet every piece of fabric at the fair. Why can't you go watch the joust like a normal person?"

"See!" she shouted at Lochlan while gesturing at Bryce.

Lochlan cleared his throat as he felt sorry for the lad and grateful that he'd only had brothers. "Aye, lass, I see quite clearly. Bryce, hie yourself to the lists. I'll take over the guardianship of your sister for you."

One would have thought the boy had just been crowned king by the look of relief and joy on his face. "May God bless you, Lord Lochlan. Your kindness truly knows no boundaries and I am sure the Lord will be merciful to you always. Truly, you have just bought yourself sainthood."

Then the boy shot off so quickly that Lochlan didn't even have a chance to respond.

Julia let out an audible sound of relief before she closed the distance between them and took his arm. "Thank you, my lord. You have truly saved my sanity this day . . . and most likely my brother's life. For my next stop had I not found you was surely at an armorer's booth for a dagger to stab him with."

"Then I'm most glad you found me."

Laughing, she released his arm and flounced off before him so that she could stop and browse at more cloth.

Graham MacKaid stepped back into the shadows as he saw Lochlan pass by and bumped into his brother Sean who was directly behind him.

"So we have two women to choose from," Sean whispered. "Which one do we take?"

"The one without a brother to back him."

Sean started away from him, but Graham grabbed his arm. "Not yet. We haven't been following him all this time to act quickly now and risk losing all. Let's find out more about the woman with him, then we'll take her."

Graham paused as another thought occurred to him. It was so evil, it made him smile. "Or better yet. Let us use that brother, shall we?"

"Use him how?"

"Remember the MacAllister was accused of killing his lover in England?"

"Aye."

"What if another young woman is found battered and raped with a bit of MacAllister plaid in her hand?"

Sean laughed. "They'll hang Lochlan for sure."

Graham nodded. "And then their clan will be divided over who should lead them. Let the MacAllister brothers fight it out. It'll be a perfect chance to show the crown what they're made of and regain our honor." He pulled his brother away from the crowd. "Tonight we'll take the girl while she sleeps."

Sean laughed. "And come the morrow, Lochlan MacAllister hangs."

Chapter 9

By the time Lochlan returned Julia to the tent she was sharing with Catarina, he completely understood why Bryce had sought a reprieve. She really had gone booth to booth, touching everything, ooohing and aahing. Sometimes even shrieking in delight. But he'd enjoyed watching her. She took so much pleasure in the smallest of things and that reminded him of Catarina, which made him ache for a taste of Catarina.

Since the moment he'd rescued her, Catarina seemed to stay on his mind whether he wanted her there or not. And the taste of her lips hung heavy on his own.

Trying to get his thoughts away from that venue and the painful need he had to sample more of Catarina than just her mouth, he deposited Julia in her tent, then headed toward his own to rest for a bit. He had to find some reprieve from his unsated lust before he lost his mind.

He was almost to his tent when someone called out to him.

Pausing, Lochlan turned to see a man old enough to be his father nearing him. He wore a fur-trimmed red surcoat and stared at him as if he were seeing a ghost. But for his life, he couldn't recall ever meeting the man before.

"May I help you?"

"You look just like a man I once knew. Giles Mac-Allister."

Well that explained it then. "That would be my father."

The man curled his lip in distaste. "And you admit it? What kind of bastard are you?"

Before he could respond, the man backhanded him a blow across his face that split open his lip.

Lochlan's temper broke. Aged or not, no one hit him in such a manner. No one. His days of tasting blood were over.

Growling, he lunged at the man, only to have someone pull him back.

"Easy, Lochlan," Bracken said in his ear. "'Tis King Henry's cousin you're about to attack. Think."

Think his arse. He wanted blood.

Still there was no tolerance in the older man's eyes as he sneered at Lochlan as if he were a leper. "I should have you arrested."

"On what grounds, my lord?" Bracken asked, tightening his hold on Lochlan, who had to force himself not to attack him for it.

"His father raped my sister."

Lochlan curled his lip. "And I am not my father."

Still, there was no reprieve in the man's eyes. "That remains to be seen. Evil like that only begets more evil in this world. I shall see to it that Lord Reginald is notified of your presence here forthwith. Were I you, I'd leave."

Bracken finally released him. "Forgive me my stupidity, my lord, but I don't understand your anger at my friend. If his father did as you say, why was he not arrested?"

The fury in his eyes was potent. "The bastard cut out her tongue and broke her arms. By the time she'd recovered enough to write down the man's name who'd assaulted her, he'd fled to Scotland, where we couldn't reach him." He spat on the ground at Lochlan's feet. "I can assure you, no one here will welcome you once I tell them who you are."

Lochlan narrowed his eyes. "Whatever lies you can live with."

"Amusing words coming from something like you." He turned and left them.

Lochlan stood silently as the revelation went through him like shattered glass. He knew his father was ruthless, but this seemed extreme even for him. The man didn't believe in sparing his fist, but this . . .

This defied cruelty and if his father had done it, then he'd have been the first to hang him for it.

Bracken met his gaze levelly. "Is what he said true?"

"I honestly don't know. My father never once spoke of such brutality and normally he bragged whenever he *punished* someone. But I can't say for certain. All I can do is hope he didn't and pray for the poor woman who was forced to suffer such monstrosity."

Lochlan couldn't stand the thought of a man capable of that fathering him. Feeling ill, he headed into his tent to try and blot the image of the unfortunate woman from his mind.

*   *   *

Cat looked up as Julia entered their tent with a bright smile on her face. "I take it you had a pleasant time?" Something she found incredulous given how much the younger woman fought with her brother.

"Oh you can't imagine," Julia said breathlessly. "I take back what I said earlier about Lord Lochlan. He's a wonderful man. Truly."

Cat arched a brow at the singsong quality of the girl's voice. "Oh?"

Even giddier than before, she knelt on the floor in front of Cat and giggled. "Aye and after spending some time with him, I was thinking I might make a good wife for him."

There was no reason for those words to anger her and yet as soon as they left Julia's lips, Cat wanted to yank her hair and beat her for them.

She had to force herself not to betray those thoughts.

Julia took her hand into her own. "Do you think I could win his heart?"

"Doubtful." She cringed as she heard the hostility in her tone, but Julia didn't seem to notice. "Lochlan has already entered into negotiations with a Scottish lord for his daughter's hand."

Julia's face fell. "Has he finalized it?"

"Nay."

The joy returned instantly to her face. "Then there's hope for me. I shall make him fall in love with me and he'll forget all about that other woman. You'll see."

That was not the intended outcome Cat had been hoping for. Unable to listen to the girl lay bare her plans to seduce Lochlan, Cat picked up her gift from the bed beside her and excused herself.

She loved Julia, but this . . . This angered her to a level she would never have thought possible. The very idea of the woman with Lochlan . . .

Julia knew nothing about handling a man like him. Nothing about being a lairdess.

Still fuming, Cat had just made her way to Lochlan's tent when she saw his confrontation with the older man. Those angry, bitter words hung heavy in her ears. Just as the look of hurt and shock on Lochlan's face hung heavy in her heart.

As soon as Lochlan was in the tent, she approached Bracken slowly.

He was about to turn away when Cat stopped his retreat. "How could he be so cruel?"

The pained look on his face seared her to the spot. "I understand his anger. If something like that, God forbid, ever happened to Julia, I wouldn't rest until I made sure the person responsible was dead . . . by my hand."

She could respect that and she'd expect no less from him. "But Lochlan's innocent of it."

Bracken nodded. "Aye, but emotions seldom listen to reason."

That was true enough and well she knew it. Her uncle was forever chiding her over allowing her emotions to get the best of her.

But still, how could someone be so harsh to an innocent man whose heart was second only to his generous spirit?

Bracken dropped his gaze to the package in her hands. He quickly blanked his expression. "I'm going to find Bryce. I'll be gone for a little while."

She frowned at his strange words as he left her rather quickly. There had been a bitter note in his voice, but she wasn't sure why.

Disregarding it, she approached the tent flap. She hesitated at barging in on him. "Lochlan?"

There was only the slightest wait before she heard his deep, rumbling brogue. "Come in, Catarina."

She didn't know why the sound of her name on his lips made her tingle, but it did. She walked in to find him standing before a chair as if he'd just stood. He looked so stiff and formal. Powerful. Reserved.

And she thought of Simon's disclosure about the woman he'd loved. The woman who had betrayed him in the worst sort of way imaginable. Her throat tightened as unnamed emotions for him washed through her.

Unsure of what to say, she forced herself to approach him. "I . . . um . . . I bought this for you."

He scowled at her. "Why?"

That was a good question. Too bad she couldn't think of an equally good response.

Clearing her throat, she shrugged. "I thought you might like it."

Lochlan wasn't sure what to think as he took the small package from her hands and unwrapped it to find a carved wooden monkey. What an odd thing to give him and he couldn't fathom her reasoning. Did she think him a child? Or worse an animal like this one to be mocked?

Afraid of the answer, he met her dark gaze. "'Tis a child's toy."

"Aye," she said with an enchanting smile, "and I thought you might find it amusing since you never play."

Relieved that she wasn't mocking him after all, he smiled down at her. "Thank you, my lady. I appreciate the thought and the gift."

Cat swallowed as she watched him. The gift seemed to disturb him and she wasn't sure why.

Seeking to comfort him, she touched his hand lightly and savored the strong feel of it. "You're not your father, Lochlan."

He stiffened. "You heard?"

"I heard."

A muscle worked in his jaw as an uncomfortable wall came up between them.

It was a wall she was desperate to breach. "I don't judge you by your family, Lochlan. I never have."

His anger didn't dissipate. "It doesn't matter, does it? Now if you'll excuse me, I wish to be alone for a bit."

Cat didn't want to leave. She wanted to soothe him, but she could tell he wouldn't welcome her presence any longer. Nay, he needed his time. "I'll be in my tent if you decide you want company."

Lochlan inclined his head to her before she left.

He didn't really want her to leave. Yet at the same time there was nothing more to be said. She'd heard his shame and, honestly, he was tired of dealing with it. He did just want to be alone.

Nay, that wasn't true. He wanted Catarina with him and he wasn't even sure why.

His heart hammering, he left the tent to pursue her. However, she was nowhere to be seen. Somehow, she'd managed to vanish into the crowd. Damn, but the woman could move quite quickly when she set her mind to it.

Assuming she was indeed headed for her tent, he made his way toward it. He'd almost reached it when he heard someone shout at him.

Frowning, he turned to see the tournament marshal leading a small group of soldiers his way.

Without a word, the guards took up position before him.

Confused by their actions, he turned to the one in charge. "Is there a problem?"

"Aye. You're under arrest," he snarled as he snatched at Lochlan's sword.

His first instinct to shove the man back, Lochlan barely caught himself before he did something that would only result in worsening his situation. The guards surrounded him. He wanted to ask what the charges were, but there was no need as he already knew that answer.

Real or imagined, he was about to pay for his father's crimes.

Cat froze inside her tent as she heard a loud shout from outside. She exchanged a frown with Julia before she went to the opening to see Lochlan being arrested.

Nay . . .

She started to go outside and demand they free him, but she knew the folly of such an act. Besides, they wouldn't listen to her. She was only a woman and they were men determined to take him to the local lord.

"What on earth?" Julia asked from her side.

Cat stepped back into the tent. "We need to find Simon and Stryder." Grabbing her cloak, she covered herself before she headed toward the lists, with Julia one step behind her.

Sure enough, Lord Stryder was in his tent. She ignored the guard as she went inside without a single announcement.

Stryder was bare from the waist up as he washed himself in a large barrel.

Cat gasped at the sight of all his tawny skin before she turned around and forced Julia to follow suit. "Forgive me for interrupting you, my lord. I should have knocked or waited to be announced."

A deep laugh rumbled from behind her. "I take it you have something of great import?"

"Aye."

"Then turn around. I'm clothed now."

Cat did and saw that he now wore a simple linen tunic. The laces of which were left untied so that even clothed, there was no hiding the fact he held an extremely well defined body. Not that she was attracted to his body, she just wasn't blind to it.

"They've arrested Lord Lochlan," she announced without any kind of preamble.

He scowled at her. "They? Who is they?"

She paused as she realized she didn't really know. "I know not. They didn't say."

He took two steps toward her. "What are his charges?"

"Again, they didn't say."

He narrowed his gaze on her as if considering her nonanswers. "Interesting. Give me a moment, my lady, to finish dressing and we'll go to the castle to see what's going on."

Grateful for his help, she gave a quick curtsy. "Thank you, my lord."

Cat returned to where Val stood with a knowing grin on his face.

"Another moment, my lady, and he'd have been naked."

"You could have told me that before I entered," she snapped at the man, who was all but a giant.

"I tried, but you were hell bent to see him. Who am I to argue with a lady?"

"You're a wretched excuse for a guard," Stryder said from inside the tent.

Val shook his head. "I'll be glad when old age takes that man's hearing. It's far too sharp for my tastes."

Cat laughed before she sent Julia back to their tent and waited for Stryder to finish.

Stryder came out of the tent with a glare on his face that could have quelled the devil as he finished lacing his surcoat. "Remind me again why I tolerate you?" he asked Val.

"I saved your arse more times than you can count."

"Are we not even yet?"

"Nay. The day we become even you'll most likely kill me, so I intend to stay one step up."

Growling at him, Stryder headed for the castle. "Follow me, my lady, and let us see what this matter is over."

Lochlan stood in the empty great hall before the count of Rouen, who was an elderly man with gray hair and sharp brown eyes. His gaze was filled with contempt as he stared at him.

"What do you wish me to do with him, Oswald?" he asked the noble who'd confronted Lochlan earlier.

"Hold him hostage until his father comes for him."

Lochlan scoffed. "That would certainly be quite a wait, my lords, since my father is dead."

Oswald didn't hesitate in his venom. "Then punish him in his father's stead."

Lucky for him, the count seemed to have better sense. "I can't do that without just cause. He's a Scottish lord."

Oswald stiffened as if that offended him to the marrow of his bones. "And I'm the cousin of a king. I demand justice, Reginald. His father destroyed my sister. He took her honor, her virginity, and her tongue. For that, I want his bastard son's neck in a noose."

Lochlan ground his teeth to keep from protesting his innocence in this. It wasn't as if they didn't know. The problem was, Oswald didn't care.

"I can't hang a man for a crime his father committed."

"Then flog him for it."

Reginald gave Lochlan a measuring stare. "How do you feel about that?"

He had to ask? Was the man daft?

"I protest it. Greatly. I've done nothing to warrant such punishment."

"Nothing he's been caught for," Oswald sneered.

"But mark my words, he's guilty of something. The apple never rolls far from the tree."

In this case, it most certainly did.

Lochlan heard the door behind him open and close.

Reginald scowled as he focused his gaze over Lochlan's shoulder. "Lord Stryder. To what do I owe the honor?"

"I heard my friend had been arrested and so I came to see why."

Lochlan turned to meet the earl, then froze as he realized Catarina was with him. He hated for her to bear witness to this event. If anyone were to recognize her, she'd be in even more trouble than he was.

"This doesn't concern you," Oswald snapped at Stryder. "This is between us and as the highest-ranking noble present, I demand the MacAllister's flesh. I want twenty lashes."

Reginald let out a long sigh before he nodded. "So be it. Guards!"

Lochlan growled as the guards came to take him. He grabbed the first one to reach him and knocked him back. As he reached for the other, he heard a soft cry of alarm.

"Cease!"

No one moved.

Catarina approached Reginald and Oswald slowly, then stopped directly in front of Reginald. "I'm afraid you're mistaken, my lord."

"Mistaken how?"

She lowered her cowl so that they could see her beautiful face. "As a princess of France, *I'm* the highest-ranking noble present and I demand you release him. Immediately."

Chapter 10

Reginald and Oswald, along with the guards, immediately bowed down before her.

Lochlan was too stunned by her actions to even breathe, never mind move. In order to save him, she'd just damned herself to return to her father's custody.

Why would she do that?

"Rise," she snapped at the guards. "And remove the shackles from him. Now."

Lochlan arched a brow at her imperious tone. Not that he hadn't heard it before, it just always surprised him when it was directed at someone other than him.

"You heard the princess," Reginald said, waving them toward Lochlan. "Do as she says."

Stryder glanced at Catarina as the guards rushed to obey her. He spoke in a low tone that only Catarina and Lochlan could hear. "Seems someone omitted a vital fact earlier when we met."

Catarina shrugged nonchalantly. "I didn't think it important."

He laughed. "Aye, well everyone else does."

"'Tis only a small birth defect that is often easily hidden. Were that this was such an occasion."

"Princess," Reginald said, rising to stand before her. "I shall have a room prepared for you immediately while I send word to your father to let him know you are safe and hale. I'm truly honored to have you grace me with your presence at our most humble fair."

Cat had to bite back her sarcasm at his words. It wasn't his fault that she had no desire to be treated like royalty, any more than she wanted her father notified of her whereabouts. Lord Reginald was trying to be graceful and kind and so would she, regardless of the knot in her stomach.

"Thank you, my lord. I appreciate your hospitality." Just as she would appreciate someone knocking her against the head with a brick. She only hoped the smile she offered him didn't appear as fake as it felt.

Lochlan approached her slowly. His gratitude shone from the very depths of his pale eyes. That alone made this worth it to her. "You didn't have to do this," he whispered.

She laid her hand on his cheek. "Aye, I did. I wasn't about to let them hurt you after everything you've done for me. What's a little confinement compared to a severe beating?"

"For you, I would think worse," he whispered. It was true, but she would never let him know that.

Lochlan couldn't breathe as he saw the pain in her dark eyes. No one had ever made such a sacrifice for him. Ever.

He closed his eyes so that he could savor her touch before he covered her hand with his. Her skin was so soft, her hand so delicate and yet it set fire to him in a way no woman or touch had before. He brought her hand to his lips and placed a tender kiss on her knuckles. "Thank you, Catarina."

She inclined her head to him.

"Your Highness," Reginald said sharply before he forced them apart. "If you'll come with me . . ."

Lochlan saw the reluctance in her gaze before she pulled away. He wanted to curse as he watched her follow the men from the room.

Stryder stepped forward and drew his attention from Catarina back to him. "Well now, here I thought I'd be the one to save your hide."

He scoffed. "I didn't think anyone could spare me what they intended."

But one thing was certain, he was going to find a way to spare Catarina from her father's plans.

Simon shook his head as he, Stryder, and Bracken stood in Stryder's tent, across from Lochlan. "You cannot break her out of the castle, Lochlan. That's kidnapping . . . and suicide. They'll hang you for it."

Those words did nothing to deter him from his plan. "They'll have to catch me to hang me."

Bracken snorted. "He's right about that and believe me, I know. But"—he cut a warning glare at Lochlan—"they will look hard and won't stop. Trust me on that, too."

Stryder made a sound of disgust in the back of his throat as he moved to pour himself another cup of mead. "Bracken is absolutely right. You take her out of that castle while Oswald is there and you know he won't rest until you're dead."

And none of that mattered to him. All he cared about was keeping Catarina away from a marriage she didn't want. "I made a promise to her and I intend to fulfill it."

Simon rolled his eyes. "While that is noble, is it really worth your life? For that matter, is it worth what they might do to your people?"

Lochlan paused. Oswald did know exactly who and what he was, and it was an enormous risk he was taking. But at the same time, he knew how much Catarina loathed being in their hands. How could he abandon her to that?

He looked at Bracken and remembered the story of her as a child, being beaten in order to force her submission.

Most of all, he remembered the way she'd looked when she'd handed him her gift.

And in that moment, his course was set in stone. "Aye, it's worth my life. I'm a man of honor and I will not see her punished for helping me. Ever."

Bracken gave a reluctant nod. "You know I'm at your back . . . so long as we're not heading to England anyway. I'd go with you even there if I didn't have two people who depended on me for their support."

Lochlan could respect that. If he had any better sense, he wouldn't be doing this either. He was about to go up against a king, swipe a princess, in the country that her father ruled, and try to take her to another against her father's wishes.

No doubt there was a special corner of hell reserved for fools like him.

Simon gave a bitter laugh. "You can count me in, too. I just have to go tell my wife what I'm about so that she doesn't banish me from our bedroom for all eternity when she wakes and finds me gone." He indicated Julia and Bryce, who were sitting off in a corner in complete silence. "You can leave them in her custody. As soon as the tourney ends, she was heading to Scotland anyway. We can rendezvous there."

Lochlan couldn't believe Simon, Stryder, and Bracken were in this with him. Were they out of their skulls? They had as much to lose, if not more, than he did. "This is more than I can ask any of you to do."

"Nay," Simon said with a laugh, "we've all . . ." he paused before he continued, "well, *I*, for one, have certainly done far more foolish things for causes nowhere near this noble."

Stryder nodded. "Likewise."

Perhaps, but Lochlan was grateful to them more than he could ever express with something as meager as words. "My thanks."

After clapping him on the back, Simon left to speak to his wife while Lochlan stared at Stryder, whose eyes accused him of all manner of stupidity. The sad part was that he agreed completely. What he planned *was* stupid.

And at the same time he couldn't make himself let it go.

Catarina needed him and he couldn't bear the thought of disappointing her.

"You know," Bracken said, "it never ceases to amaze me the things men will do for the love of a woman."

"I'm not in love with her."

Bracken scoffed. "Of course you're not. Why else would you risk this?"

"I made a promise." But even he was beginning to doubt his conviction. The truth was Catarina meant a lot more to him than she should have.

"I think it's romantic," Julia said dreamily. "It makes Lord Lochlan a true and decent hero." She leveled a meaningful glare at Bryce. "Would that all men were so noble."

Bryce groaned as if her words cut through him. "Careful, Lord Lochlan, I fear my sister may have set her sights on your hand."

Julia slapped playfully at her brother. "You're such an unfeeling cad."

"And you're a ninny."

"And the both of you are annoying," Bracken snapped. "For the love of God and all his saints, hie yourselves to Simon's tent and pester his wife while we think without your mewling voices and petty arguments."

Both Julia and Bryce looked highly offended. For the first time, they locked arms in a unified front, lifted their chins haughtily in the air, and left the tent.

"Good job," Stryder said to Bracken. "Thought I was going to have to kill one or the other."

"Please don't. For all their trying ways, they are the only thing I have left in this world that means anything to me. As much as they irritate me, I would truly miss them if they were gone."

Stryder laughed. "As an older brother, father, and husband myself, I completely understand."

Bracken let out an appreciative breath. "'Tis a wonder you haven't thrown yourself from the nearest turret given that load."

"There are times . . ." Stryder turned his gaze to Lochlan. "Then again, it appears I am definitely a bit suicidal to join in on this crusade."

Lochlan joined his laughter. "Aye and when they lead me toward the gallows, remind me again that I did this for honor."

Bracken scoffed. "I still say you're doing this for love, but every time I say it you dismiss me."

"And still do." But the more he denied it, the more he wondered if he wasn't protesting too much. His heart did soften at the thought of Catarina and with her absence there was an ache inside him that he didn't even want to contemplate. It was as if a part of him were missing.

That was ridiculous. Catarina annoyed him to the core of his soul. She insulted him.

She'd *bitten* him.

Yet he considered her a friend. One he was willing to risk his life and his clan for.

Aye, there was something wrong with him, no doubt.

Cat tried to focus on what Lady Anabeth was saying as a small group of women sat sequestered in a sewing circle in the lady's solar, but honestly she couldn't. It was something to do with the trim of her gown or perhaps a gown someone else wore. The woman rattled on without pausing even to breathe. In all her life she'd never seen anything like it.

Mayhap she should have allowed Lochlan to be beaten after all . . .

But even as she thought that she knew better.

What was a little boredom compared to what they would have done to him?

Still the lady droned on in her high, nasal tone about something garish.

Then again . . .

"Princess?"

She looked up at the young maid who was bowing before her. "Please rise, child."

The girl did, then handed her a small piece of paper. "I was bid by a gentleman to give this to you, Your Highness."

"Thank you."

The girl bowed again before she left the room.

"Is it a love note?" Lady Anabeth asked breathlessly, as all the women stared at her as if she held the grail.

Cat somehow doubted it. Who on earth would send her such? A hate note, she'd believe in an instant. But it did make her curious.

Opening it, she had to force her eyes not to bulge.

My dearest,

Meet me at midnight out in the gardens and I shall make all your dreams come true.

Lochlan

She had to read it three times more to make sure her mind wasn't playing a trick on her. She couldn't imagine Lochlan writing something like that.

It was so . . .

Poetic. Gentle. Tender.

So extremely unlike him. Perhaps it was his idea of a jest? He did have an odd sense of humor. However, she understood the sentiment. If he was indeed planning to rescue her, she couldn't be more grateful.

God bless the man. Then again, it was the least he could do given that she wouldn't be in this predicament without him.

"What does it say?" Anabeth leaned forward, trying to read it.

Cat smiled as she folded it carefully, then tucked it between her breasts so that one of the nosey ladies wouldn't find it. "It appears to be a lover's note after all."

The women gave a collective gasp.

"Who?" the small blond beside her asked.

"A secret admirer."

Anabeth's eyes bulged. "Really? Who do you think he could be?"

"I vote for Lord Stryder." Lucinda giggled from beside Anabeth. "He would make a most splendid lover."

"Shh," Anabeth said, placing her forefinger to her lips. "Lady Rowena would have your tongue if she ever heard that."

"Aye, but I envy her." Lucinda looked around. "And I know I'm not the only woman here who feels that way."

The entire group broke out into a round of wicked giggles.

Cat rose from her chair while the women speculated on the virtues of the knights who were competing and tried to guess who among them would have sent a note to her. Little did they know not a one of those men held her heart.

It seemed to beat only for a rigid man whose brogue was as thick as a Scotsman's porridge. She ran her hand over the front of her gown so that she could feel his letter there. For the first time since she was led to her prison, she was relieved and when next she saw Lochlan, she would make sure he knew exactly how grateful she was for his kindness.

Hours seemed to have dragged on into infinity before Cat was able to head down to the great hall below to partake of supper. Of course Reginald insisted that she sit at his table up on the dais and away from the other nobles. The only thing that made it bearable was the presence of Rowena.

Unfortunately, the countess sat on the other side of a rather rude, boisterous earl who kept sucking his wine through his teeth.

If I do have to marry the prince, please don't let that be one of his habits.

Cat would slit her wrists before she condemned herself to another meal with such a man. The best she could do was lean forward and wave at Rowena.

Sighing, she leaned back in her chair as she watched the other nobles at the lower tables eating while the musicians filled the room with soothing melody. Servants came and went as she picked at her food and swept the hall looking for a certain blond warrior.

He was nowhere to be seen and that saddened her.

Where are you, Lochlan?

Perhaps he was planning their escape even as she sat here. They would have to be careful since Oswald knew him and hated him.

Maybe Lochlan has forgotten me.

Now that was a foolish thought. He wouldn't be so cruel as to send her his note, then not follow through.

The waiting, though, was even more torturous than the man sucking wine beside her. She could swear a full decade had passed before the meal finished and the servants began clearing tables and moving them so that people could dance.

Cat left the area and headed down toward the crowd in search of Lochlan or Bracken.

"Would you care to dance, Highness?"

She looked over her shoulder to find a tall, handsome knight smiling at her. Around her own age, he had jolly blue eyes and dark brown hair. There was an air of charitable humor to him.

"Aye, my lord, thank you."

He inclined his head before he held his hand out to her. Taking his proffered hand, she followed him to the floor so that they could dance.

"Do you have a name, sir knight?" she asked, as they took up position with the other dancers.

"Frederick, Your Highness. Baron of Chantilier."

She'd never heard of that place. "'Tis an honor to dance with you, my lord."

"And with you, Highness."

She inclined her head to him before the dance began. They didn't have an opportunity to speak too much more as they weaved between the others and passed partners. Cat continued to search the crowd for Bracken or Lochlan.

But again, she was disappointed. Not even Simon was around. Where could they all be?

Lochlan froze as he entered the hall and saw the dancers on the floor. In truth, there was only one dancer who drew and captured his gaze immediately and she was the most graceful of all. Every arc of her arm, every step of her foot was a symphony. Surely the woman had to be descended directly from a muse to possess that much talent. There was no other explanation.

And when he saw her smile at the stranger she was dancing with an unwarranted fury assaulted him. Never in his life had he wanted to kill anyone as much as he wanted to kill that unnamed man.

Before he could think better of it, he was across the room and cutting in.

Cat looked up with a gasp as she finally saw the one person she'd been seeking.

"May I?"

Lord Frederick graciously backed away.

Cat couldn't breathe as she saw the look of furious pain on Lochlan's face. "Are you going to dance with me?" she asked, hoping to lighten his mood a trifle.

"If I must."

The reluctance in his tone was enough to make her merciful toward him. She took his hand and led him away from the other dancers.

Lochlan let out a relieved breath that she hadn't forced him to dance. "Thank you for not embarrassing me."

Her smile literally took his breath away. "It's the least I can do for the man who intends to relieve me of my current predicament."

Lochlan smiled at her words as he continued to hold her hand. "So you received my message?"

"Aye and it couldn't have come at a better time. I was already near madness." She closed her eyes and drew in a deep breath as if savoring the thought. "Thank you."

He tsked at her as he led her outside to a small garden that was just off the hall. "Do you think me such a villain that I'd leave you to your worst nightmare after you saved me?"

"Honestly, I've known many who would have. But nay, I expected you to come for me."

"Then I'm grateful I didn't disappoint you."

Cat paused by a bench to look up at him. In the moonlight, he was so incredibly handsome. Then again, he was always handsome, no matter the light. There was just something about the moon that softened his features and made him appear less harsh and stern. Her heart pounding, she wanted to taste him.

She rose up slowly.

Lochlan let out a feral growl before he pulled her against him and kissed her breathless. She should have no feeling for this man and yet she did. All she wanted was to hold him close. To keep him right here, in her arms. She didn't know why, but she drew strength from him. Comfort.

And she never wanted to leave that.

But the most surprising thing she felt was the foreign sensation of being home. It was as if she were meant to be in his arms.

Closing her eyes, she breathed him in.

Lochlan cupped her head in his hands as desire flooded his body. In all his life, he'd never ached like this for a woman. He wanted her in a way that defied any reason. He was about to do something for her that he'd sworn he'd never do for anyone.

Jeopardize his people. Risk his life.

And he didn't even care. Nay it wasn't that, he did care. But keeping her safe was even more important to him.

Someone cleared their throat.

Lochlan pulled back to find Lord Reginald scowling at them.

"Your Highness?" the man said coldly.

Cat blinked her eyes open. Instead of looking behind her to see Reginald, she continued to look up at Lochlan. The innocent desire he saw reflected in her eyes tore through him like fire. Whatever this madness that had possession of him had also taken her.

"Highness," Reginald practically barked. "I think it best you return inside."

"Don't forget me," she mouthed the words to him.

"Never," he breathed.

Her smile floored him before she pulled away and turned to follow Reginald back inside. Lochlan stood there, his heart aching from the loss.

"You are a brave man."

He turned at the deep voice that was coming out of the darkness behind him. He could make out only the faintest outlines of the man's body. "How so?"

Damien St. Cyr stepped out of the shadows to eye him coldly. As before, his face was concealed by a silver mask, which made Lochlan wonder if the man wasn't infected with leprosy. "You dabble with a princess when half her father's court is in attendance. What else could you possibly be?"

"Foolish."

Damien let out a low laugh. "Aye, of that I have no doubt. I will say this though, my cousin doesn't trust anyone and yet she followed you out here. I find that . . . odd."

"Is that why you were spying on us?"

Damien smirked. "Nay. I was here already. You two disturbed the fresh air I was trying to find."

"Then I shall leave you to it." He started back for the hall.

"Lochlan?"

He paused at Damien's call. "Aye?"

"A word to the wise. There are enemies aplenty here."

His blood ran cold at the warning. "Meaning what?"

Damien brushed his bottom lip with his thumb as if considering how to respond. When he did, his voice was laden with warning. "A good friend once told me to be wary where you put your trust. Not everyone is as careful with it as you are." And with that he vanished back into the shadows.

Lochlan stood there, contemplating those words. They were wise indeed, but he wondered what had prompted them. He was still frowning when he returned to the great hall.

A quick scan failed to locate Catarina. But Simon joined him almost as soon as he returned.

"Are you all right?" Simon asked.

"Aye. I just had a strange encounter."

Simon's eyes widened. "Are you speaking of your tryst with Catarina?"

Lochlan scowled. "I beg your pardon?"

"That was on the tongue of many a wagging gossipmonger when I arrived. It appears you were seen kissing Catarina outside in the gardens."

Lochlan let out a sound of disgust. "Nay. Have they nothing better to do?"

"Than ruin lives for no other reason than they can? Nay. 'Tis the nature of people, I fear, to speak out of turn and harshly about those they don't know."

Truer words were never spoken.

Simon cleared his throat. "Well if you aren't speaking of the gossips, then what has you scowling so?"

"I spoke to Damien St. Cyr outside. He told me to be wary of my trust. That others wouldn't be as careful with it as I."

"Hmmm."

There was something hidden in that idle comment. "What?"

Simon folded his arms over his chest. "I find it odd myself. 'Tis something Stryder used to say when we were youths together."

Hmmm indeed. That was interesting. "You think it a threat against Stryder?"

"With Damien, one never knows. Something truly horrible happened to him in the Holy Land. He didn't come back intact and I don't mean just his face was disfigured. Methinks his mind as well."

"Disfigured?"

He nodded. "It's why he wears his mask. Apparently the Saracens tortured him and his face was destroyed. To my knowledge no one has seen it since he returned."

So that explained it. "I thought he had leprosy."

"Nay. But from the tales that are told, he would probably prefer that."

No doubt. Lochlan let out a tired breath as he scanned the crowd again seeking a dark, slight form.

"If you're seeking our lady, they took her above as soon as she entered the room. Most likely to get her away from . . . oh what term did the crone use? Your most lecherous lips."

He cringed at Simon's teasing. "Is that supposed to make me feel better?"

Simon grinned playfully. "Nay, I was hoping to incense you."

"For any particular reason?"

"My nature. Now if you'll excuse me, I see my lady wife is attempting to climb out of her chair. Let me go assist her."

Lochlan watched as Simon rushed across the hall to a petite but plain woman. Her features softened the moment she saw him and the love in her expression made his own chest tighten. He would give anything to have a woman look at him like that.

Just once.

Simon kissed her hand before he practically picked her up out of her chair and set her on her feet. Offering her his arm, he escorted her to the stairs.

Lochlan glanced up to the ceiling above his head as he wondered where Catarina was and what she was doing. He felt her absence like a physical pain.

But they would be together again soon enough. Holding close to that thought, he made his way back toward his tent.

Cat couldn't stop pacing as time once again dragged on unmercifully. It really was true that time only passed swiftly when one enjoyed oneself. If one were suffering, it lagged like the weakest of snails.

But finally midnight came.

Relieved, she used the pretext of needing to go to the garderobe to get past her guards and Reginald's wife. As soon as she was certain they weren't following her, she diverted her course toward the gardens where she'd left Lochlan earlier.

The moon had fallen behind a cloud, making the entire area dark and spooky. Her imagination went wild with seeing demons and wolves in every shadow.

Or worse someone who would call out to the guards to take her.

She moved slowly and with purpose until she was back at the very spot where they'd stood earlier.

Her heart hammering, she tried to peer through the darkness to find her champion. *Where are you, Lochlan?* The question chased itself around in her mind until she felt a presence behind her.

She turned toward it with a smile . . . one that faded as soon as she could see the man's face.

It wasn't Lochlan.

Terrified, she started to move away only to run into another man's body. Tall and broadshouldered, he looked down at her with an evil glint in his eye.

"Evening, Princess."

Before she could move, he stuffed a cloth in her mouth and wrapped a rope around her body. She tried to scream and kick, but they seemed to expect it.

The next thing she knew, they'd covered her head with a sack and had her completely tied up.

"She may not have a brother to demand his life, but methinks the king will be sure to kill Lochlan for us. Now leave the cloth and let us go."

Chapter 11

Lochlan frowned as he continued to wait for Catarina in the shadows by the stairs. She should have been here long ago. Something was wrong. He knew it.

Worried, he headed outside to where Simon and Stryder were waiting for them so that they could take Catarina to safety. "She hasn't shown."

Simon looked to Stryder. "You did tell her the stairs, correct?"

"Me?" he asked, aghast. "I thought *you* were to tell her."

Simon snorted. "Nay. I distinctly remember

we decided *you* would be the one to give her the meeting time and place."

"No one informed me of this. Last word to me was that you would be the one to speak to her."

A bad feeling went through Lochlan. "She told me after supper that she'd received my message."

Stryder scowled. "Did she say who'd given it to her?"

He shook his head.

A muscle worked in Simon's jaw. "Do you think Bracken could have told her?"

Lochlan doubted it. "Since Bracken was taking your lady wife home, nay. I didn't give him the location for fear of endangering them."

Stryder cursed. "Then who did she speak to?"

"That would be the question . . ." Along with who else would have known about their plans. Lochlan scanned the area, but there was no sign of her anywhere.

Stryder stepped back. "I'll have Rowena check her room. Maybe she's still there. Something could have happened. Perhaps she couldn't get past the guards."

That would definitely make Lochlan feel better. He wanted to believe that she was still safe and sound in her room. "I'll wait here until your return." But that was the last thing he wanted to do.

He felt the need to start searching for her immediately. Every second they delayed, could be critical to her well-being if she wasn't there.

"I'll check the stables for her horse," Simon said. "And if it's still there, I'll check the stairs again."

"My thanks."

Lochlan paced the small area while a million scenarios went through his head. Part of them revolved around Catarina running on her own from them, but she'd seemed content enough that he and the others would take her from here.

Had someone kidnapped her for ransom? It was possible and frightening.

After several minutes, he paused in his pacing as he saw Stryder approaching with a stern grimace on his face. "She wasn't there. Rowena found this in her room." He held out a piece of folded vellum.

Lochlan opened it and read the note that was signed with his name and as he did so, fury sizzled through him. Who the devil would have used his name? "I didn't write this."

"We figured as much. Rowena said that it was left out in the open as if someone had meant for it to be seen. If Cat had truly gone to meet you as planned, she wouldn't have left anything behind to incriminate you in the deed."

That was true enough. "Who could have left it, then?"

Stryder shrugged. "I'm sure whoever sent it to her. Have you any enemies?"

Lochlan snorted at the obvious answer to that. "Oswald."

"True, but I don't think his hatred would cause him to risk his own life. If the king finds out his daughter has been taken against her will and his, the culprit will die."

True enough. This newest deed defied logic, but then people seeking vengeance often did things that made no sense. "Someone is after me and I'm willing to wager whoever it is will kill her for it."

"I agree."

Terror for what they might be doing to her even while he spoke to Stryder invaded every part of him. "We have to find her as soon as possible."

"Aye and I know just the person who can help us." Stryder motioned him to follow as he turned and made his way back to the tents where the knights were camped.

Lochlan scowled but didn't speak. Why would they come here and not set out immediately?

But he knew enough to trust the earl.

After a few minutes, they reached a tent that was set apart from the others, on the outer edge of the field. It was all black. Stryder motioned him to silence before he parted the flap. There was a small lamp burning inside that illuminated a pallet on the floor where a lean man lay sleeping. Lochlan grimaced at the harsh scars marring the man's flesh. He had long brown hair that fell over his face, obscuring his features.

Black armor was set to the opposite side of the tent on a dummy. And by the red and gold markings on the man's black shield, it was obvious he was a bastard-born mercenary with no lands or title.

Yet there was no sign of a sword or dagger.

Stryder approached the sleeping man but before he could touch him, the man awoke. Cursing, he swung his arm out and it wasn't until Stryder caught his hand that Lochlan realized the man held a dagger that would have slit Stryder's throat had he not expected and countered the attack.

"It's me, Kestrel. Relax."

He wrenched his arm free of Stryder's grip. "You know better than to wake me."

"I know, but I need your help."

Kestrel narrowed his suspicious gaze on Lochlan. "Since he stands at your back, I'm assuming he's a friend."

"Aye. He was traveling with the French prin-

cess and now she's been taken. It appears whoever took her is trying to blame it on him."

Kestrel clenched his teeth, then nodded. "I'll be
dressed and ready to travel in three shakes."

Stryder released his hand. "Thank you."

Kestrel gave a subtle nod before he brought his
sword out from under the blanket.

Stryder straightened up and led Lochlan from
the tent. They stood off to the side to give the
man privacy while he dressed. "He's a bit harsh
at times," Stryder said in a low, apologetic tone.
"But he's had a hard past."

"Can we trust him?"

"I'd put my life in his hands."

There was no better statement than that. "He
was with you in Outremer?"

Stryder nodded. "After we escaped and he returned home to his family, his father disowned
him."

Lochlan was stunned by that. "Why?"

"Because he returned and his older brother
didn't."

That made no sense to him, but having had a father who would have most likely reacted the same
way, he understood. "Was he bastard born?"

Stryder shook his head. "But none of his family
is allowed even to speak his name. So he wears

the mark of a bastard and refuses to acknowledge any of them. He won't even use his given name anymore."

Lochlan felt for the poor man.

He started to speak, then paused as Kestrel joined them. His long hair was pulled back at his neck and stubble marred his otherwise perfect goatee. He was dressed in a black pair of breeches and a plain black surcoat. The only thing to mark him as a knight was the sword he wore and an air of competent death that surrounded him.

Kestrel approached them with determination. "What do you need?"

"We have no trace of the princess," Stryder said. "You're the only man I know who can track them."

One corner of Kestrel's mouth quirked up in a deadly smile. "Do you have anything?"

Stryder handed him the vellum. "Only this note."

Kestrel looked at it without taking it. "What does it say?"

Realizing the man was illiterate, which wasn't uncommon for a knight, Lochlan read it to him.

Kestrel nodded. "Follow me, my lords. We're going to find the bastard who took her and kill him."

* * *

Why does this feel so familiar? Unfortunately Cat knew the answer. Every time she turned around, it seemed some man was tying her up to take her someplace she didn't want to be.

The only difference now was that these men intended to kill her and blame Lochlan for it.

Growling deep in her throat, she worked against the ropes that held her hands together. She was getting really tired of having chafe marks and rope burns on her wrists.

"I say we should go ahead and kill her," Graham MacKaid said to his brother.

"Nay, not yet. We have to give Lochlan enough time to vanish as well. If it appears she's been murdered while he's still in camp with those who can verify his whereabouts, they'll know he didn't kill her. We have to send the note to him and have him come for her, then we kill her and everyone will think he did it."

"Keeping her alive makes me nervous."

"She's a woman. What can she do?"

If she wasn't bound and gagged, she'd be more than willing to show him just how far from helpless she was. As it was, all she could do was glare at them and hope she freed herself before their brother returned and told them Lochlan had left the camp.

Graham turned toward her and scowled.

Cat stopped moving.

But it was too late. He'd seen what she was about. He sneered as he approached her. "You think you can untie that, Princess?"

Honestly, aye. She'd untied a lot better knots than this one.

But she wasn't about to tell him what she thought. When dealing with an enemy, silence was indeed the greatest virtue. They should never know what their opponent was thinking.

So she returned his sneer with one of her own. Not that it was probably off-putting given the fact that she was gagged, but it at least made her feel better.

Graham scoffed at her. "She doesn't look very regal, does she?"

"Nay. More like a peasant. Even in finery, I'd have never guessed her breeding."

As if their breeding was any better. What kind of man trussed a woman up like this, then butchered her while she was helpless?

Where were her father's guards when she needed them?

Graham fingered his knife while he watched her. "Have no fear, Princess. We'll make the cut clean. There won't be much pain before you die."

Well that just made her feel all better about it. But even with her inner quips, the truth was she was scared. Terribly. If she didn't get out of this, she would die. Alone and painfully. There was no reprieve from these monsters. They were determined to end her life.

Truthfully, she didn't want this. There was so much more she'd wanted to do with her life. She wanted . . .

Lochlan. She didn't know why he'd be her last thought, but he was. He would agonize over this and she didn't want to add that pain to him. He'd hold himself responsible.

And it wasn't just that. She wanted to see him again. To touch him. He truly was her biggest regret. She wouldn't be here to see him find his brother.

She wouldn't . . .

Cat stopped her maudlin thoughts and sniffed at the tears that were stinging her eyes. This wasn't her. She would not give up or in to these cretins. Not so long as there was a single breath in her body. Lochlan didn't deserve the fate these animals had planned for him and neither did she.

Nay, she would survive this and as Lochlan would say, they'd both play a giddy tune over their graves.

Her anger renewed, she kicked out against her captor. He yelped before he fell to the ground. Cat pushed herself up and tried to run, but the other one caught her about the waist and threw her down.

She tried to kick him, too, but he was smarter than Graham.

"You do that again, lass, and I'll cut your leg off."

Cat slammed her head against the ground in frustration as he moved to tie her feet. She tried to kick, but it didn't do any good. Now she was trussed up so that she truly had no other hope.

Closing her eyes, she prayed with renewed vigor. This couldn't be the end of her. It couldn't.

Lochlan watched as Kestrel kept low to the ground and examined every part of the garden. "What is he doing?"

"He's reading the foliage."

"How so?"

"I have no idea. 'Twas a game his uncle would play with him and his brother. He taught them to track better than any hound or hawk I've ever seen."

Simon smiled as he came up behind them. "Kestrel. I should have known."

Kestrel looked up with a feral grimace. "Would you old maids stop your chattering? I'm trying to concentrate."

Lochlan wasn't sure he believed in the man's abilities, until he rejoined them. "There were three men who took her." He held out a piece of plaid and velvet. "They left this behind to be found."

Lochlan cursed at the sight. "'Tis a plaid my brothers and I use."

Simon cursed. "They're setting you up."

"Aye and this confirms it."

"Can you find their trail?" Stryder asked Kestrel.

A slow smile spread over Kestrel's face. "One isn't far from here," he whispered. "He's waiting on us to leave Lochlan alone methinks."

"How do you know that?"

"I know how a cruel mind works. And I know how to make an innocent man look guilty. We need to get to the lady quickly before they harm her."

"Lead on," Lochlan said.

But Kestrel didn't move. "We could do that, my lords. But truthfully, I have a much better plan."

Chapter 12

"Where the devil is Sean?" Graham snarled, as he and his brother waited by the fire like two unholy demons plotting an attack. "Lochlan should be alone by now. I don't understand what's keeping him."

Cat let out a slow breath. She had to get away from them. The sooner, the better.

She paused as a thought occurred to her. Smiling, she started speaking around her gag.

The two of them glared at her. With a snarl contorting his face, Graham came forward to remove her gag.

She forced herself to appear sweet and innocent.

"I realize that this is probably an inconvenient time, but I fear you must loosen me."

Graham snorted. "And why would we do that?"

"So that I don't soil my clothing"—she glanced toward a clump of bushes—"if you take my meaning and being as intelligent as you are, I'm sure you do."

Graham curled his lip at her. "You deserve the death I'm going to give you."

Cat didn't respond as he moved forward to loosen her feet so that she could stand. The urge to kick him was so strong, she wasn't sure how she curbed the impulse, but kicking him would only get her feet tied again and that wouldn't allow her to run from him.

She held her arms toward him. "What of my hands?"

"What of them?"

"I can't very well hold my gown while tied like this, now can I?"

His brother raked her with a speculative sneer. "We could send her naked."

Graham laughed before he grabbed at her skirt.

Cat shrieked in outrage and tried to push him away. He grabbed her by the hair and wrenched her head as hard as he could.

She drew back to kick him, then paused as an

arrow went whizzing past her head, straight into Graham's shoulder. Screaming, he fell back. She ducked and headed in the opposite direction.

But she didn't get far before a man stopped her. She growled low in her throat, intending to fight until she looked up.

Her heart stopped as she met Lochlan's gaze. The relief and adoration there stole her breath. He crushed her against him before he kissed her with more passion than she'd known existed. She savored the taste of him for as long as she could before he pulled away and left her with a curse so profane it made her blush.

She turned in time to see Graham coming at them with a raised dagger. Faster than she could blink, Lochlan was around her. He caught Graham's wrist and in one fluid movement, he twisted the dagger from his hand and punched him straight in the face.

But that wasn't enough for him. Lochlan threw the dagger to the ground and continued to beat Graham, who was no longer able to defend himself from the forceful blows that kept him reeling. It was so uncharacteristic of Lochlan that all she could do was gape. He was always so controlled, so proper, that this side of him actually frightened her.

"Lochlan!" Stryder snapped before he pulled him back. "He's had enough. You're going to kill him."

Still, Lochlan kicked out at Graham, catching him against the ribs before Stryder forced him away.

Lying on the ground, bleeding profusely, Graham spat at him.

Lochlan lunged for him, only to have Stryder and another man block his way.

"See to Catarina," Stryder ordered fiercely.

His breathing ragged, Lochlan continued to glare at Graham as if he could tear him to pieces. He pulled out a small dagger and cut the rope from her wrists.

Her entire body shaking, Cat placed her hand on his shoulder. Lochlan turned toward her then and the feral light in his pale eyes made her shiver. Without a word, he picked her up in his arms and held her so tightly that she could barely breathe.

An unbridled giddiness filled her at his actions. He didn't care that the others were watching or that what he did was highly improper. He was glad she was safe and he didn't mind showing it to all of them. She wrapped her arms around his shoulders and buried her face against his neck so that she could inhale his warm scent.

"Damn, who tore him up?" She heard Simon's voice from behind them.

Stryder snorted. "That would be Lochlan. Apparently he didn't like the way they'd treated his lady."

Simon laughed. "Then let me mark upon my memory to always treat the fair Catarina with only the highest regard . . . and very gentle gloves."

Cat placed a light kiss to Lochlan's cheek. "Are you going to set me back on my feet?"

His arms tightened around her. "Nay, lass. Every time I set you loose, you find nothing but trouble. 'Tis a wonder your uncle didn't put chains on you."

She laughed at his words. It was true. Bavel had threatened her with such repeatedly. "I fear your arms will eventually tire of me."

He pulled back from her and the look in his eyes said that he'd never tire of her. But for the first time he became aware of the other lords staring curiously at them.

She swore she could feel his reluctance as he finally put her feet on the ground and released his hold. An inexplicable emptiness filled her.

At least until he quietly took her hand into his. That single action brought tears to her eyes as tenderness flooded her heart and made it pound ever harder.

Stryder cleared his throat. "We're going to see

these bastards into custody. Why don't you and Catarina go on ahead. We'll rendezvous at the boat in Honfleur later today."

She was surprised when none of the men made an effort to come with them. Rather they all followed after Stryder while Lochlan gently pulled her toward their horses.

The men left so quickly she would have thought the devil himself was after them. "How very odd."

Lochlan didn't seem as perturbed by their behavior. "More astute, I'd say."

"How so?"

His answer came in the form of a kiss so hot it melted her and left her clinging to him. She couldn't think as he literally devoured her mouth. She buried one hand in his hair to steady herself as his tongue danced with hers.

Lochlan knew he shouldn't be kissing her like this. She was a princess, but honestly he didn't give a flying monk's arse. All that mattered to him was that she was safe and in his arms.

The terror of thinking her gone . . .

Then seeing her face where she'd obviously been struck by those bastards. Never in his life had he felt such fury toward anyone. Had Stryder not stopped him, he would have knifed Graham where he lay and not even cared.

Now to have her back . . . All he wanted was to taste her. To touch her skin and breathe her in.

His heart hammering, he pulled back to look down at her. She blinked open her eyes and the passion he saw there seared him.

He took the hand she still had buried in his hair and brought it to his lips so that he could nibble her fingers. "I want you, Catarina," he said, his tone low and guttural. "I've no right to ask it of you, but I—"

She cut his words off with a kiss of her own. Lochlan smiled as she literally assaulted his lips with her eagerness. He scooped her up in his arms and carried her away from the horses, to a secluded spot that was surrounded by thick foliage.

Laying her down against the grass, he covered her with his body. Honestly, he couldn't believe she was welcoming him like this. And as he reached for the hem of her skirt, he half expected her to slap him for it.

But she didn't. She actually lifted her hips so that he could reach beneath the voluminous fabric to touch her. He swore his mouth watered as he skimmed his hand over her smooth thigh to press her closer to his body.

Cat shivered at the heat of his hand on her bare skin. No man had ever touched her there. Even though she was a virgin, she wasn't naive. She knew exactly what he sought and what she was agreeing to. Her father would be furious if he ever found out. He'd most likely kill Lochlan, but she would never betray him by telling a soul what they were doing.

This night was theirs.

Her father intended to sell her off to the highest-bidding prince and in the event she lost this one-sided fight they were having, she wanted at least one memory of being with someone *she* chose. And there was no man she'd rather have than Lochlan MacAllister.

Needing to feel closer to him, she unlaced his tunic and pulled it over his head. She sucked her breath in sharply at the sight of his bared chest. Tanned and well muscled, he was magnificent.

The sensation of his hard body on hers . . .

Surely not even heaven could be better than this.

Lochlan loosened the stays on her gown before he dipped his head to gently nuzzle the top of her breast. Moaning deep in her throat, she cradled his head against her as he finally succeeded in freeing her breasts. He laughed in triumph before he took the tip of her right breast into his mouth and suckled her gently.

Cat trembled at the sensation of his hot tongue sweeping over her nipple. The lick made her stomach contract and the center of her body throbbed painfully. She didn't understand the sensations she felt. They were hot and fierce. Frightening and exciting.

And when he dipped his hand down to touch the part of her that ached most she actually gasped out loud. She wasn't sure how to behave or what to do. All she could feel was the pleasure his fingers gave her as they swept over and into her body.

Lochlan growled deep in his throat as he toyed with her. Her fingernails bit harshly into his biceps, but he didn't care. The only thing he wanted was to taste her.

Hungry for her, he kissed his way down her stomach until he reached the center of her body. She was so incredibly beautiful with the moonlight on her face and her flesh bared to him.

He gently spread her open before he leaned down to take her into his mouth.

Cat cried out as unbelievable ecstasy tore through her. It was raw and demanding and it made her insides contract and flutter. Never in her life had she experienced anything like the feeling of his tongue swirling around her.

She wasn't sure if he was supposed to be doing this, but, truthfully, she didn't want him to stop. It was enough to make her fear for her very sanity.

And just when she reached the point she didn't think she could stand anymore, her body ruptured.

Throwing her head back, she screamed out as her body felt like it was coming undone. Waves and waves of pleasure spiraled through her one after another. It was absolutely frightening.

"Lochlan? What did you do to me?"

He gave her one long lick before he nipped her inner thigh. "That is an orgasm, lass, and that is why men are willing to lay their lives down to have a woman."

She certainly could understand wanting to feel it. But she wasn't so sure it was worth her life. "Did you . . . ?"

He laughed. "Nay, love. I'm still not sated."

Biting her lip, she watched as he loosened his breeches. And when he lowered them to free his shaft, she couldn't help but stare at him. He was huge and it scared her. Surely her body couldn't accommodate *that*.

His eyes hot, he took her hand into his and guided it to him. The softness of him amazed her. He was so hard and yet it was like stroking velvet.

But it was the pleasure on his face that pushed her fear away. Lochlan wouldn't hurt her. She knew that.

He pushed her skirt up to her waist before he moved himself to lie between her spread legs. The tip of him was pressed against her. He dipped his head down to seize her lips into a sizzling kiss before he pressed himself home.

Cat hissed as a raw, burning pain assailed her. "Ow!"

He cupped her head in his hands and pulled back to look down at her face. "It won't hurt for long, I promise."

She found that hard to believe. "'Tis easy for you to say. You're not the one hurting."

"Trust me, lass, I'm in pain right now, too. It's nigh killing me to not thrust against you, but I won't do that to you until you're ready for me."

And with those words spoken, he slowly nibbled her lips. Cat closed her eyes. She loved his kisses. They were tender and sweet and they set her on fire. But the rest . . .

Her thoughts scattered as he breathed against her ear and the fire inside reignited.

Before long, she forgot the pain and focused only on their combined breaths.

Lochlan ground his teeth as he finally felt her

relaxing. He hated that he'd hurt her when he entered her. What he'd done was selfish, but he couldn't help himself. She was the only thing he wanted.

All his life, he'd lived for other people, never asking anyone for anything. He'd never before taken something for himself.

But by all that was holy, he was going to take her. She was what he needed. What he craved and there was no denying the madness he felt every time she drew near.

Unable to resist her, he slowly moved against her. He half expected her to tense again, but she didn't.

Instead, she lifted her legs, pulling him even deeper inside her.

He shivered at the welcoming heat of her body. At the slick feel of her as he thrust against her.

Cat groaned as Lochlan rose up on his arms so that he could look down at her while he slid himself even deeper into her. The sight of his pleasure made her smile as she reached up to cup his face in her hand.

He dipped his head down to kiss the inside of her wrist as he quickened his strokes. This time there was no pain. All she could feel was his thickness pressing into her body and she wanted more of it. Biting her lip, she lifted her hips to help him.

He let out a sharp gasp before he lowered himself back down on top of her and cradled her against him.

And when he came, he cried out her name.

Cat held him close as she felt his heart hammering against her breasts. "Are you all right?"

He laughed softly. "I should be asking you that, lass."

"Aye, but I've never seen you so relaxed. 'Tis enough to frighten me."

He kissed her cheek before he rolled over and pulled her across him. "You are a treasure, Catarina. Forget whatever I said about restraint. I much prefer your wildness."

She frowned at him. "Have you bumped your head?"

He brushed the hair back from her face. "Nay. More like my eyes have been opened and for the first time I see things a bit more clearly."

"Such as?"

"You. I thought they were going to kill you."

It was strange how she'd gone from utter terror to the peace she felt now. "That thought occurred to me, too. But I knew you'd find me."

"Did you now?"

"Aye."

His pale eyes teased her. "And you had no doubt?"

She wrinkled her nose playfully. "Perhaps a little."

"Just a little?"

Cat nodded. "It was quickly sliding into a lot, but just as it was veering over the cliff you came and saved me. Again. Thank you, Lochlan."

He nibbled her chin. "There's nothing to thank me for. Especially not after the gift you've given me tonight."

"I'm not sure which of us received the better gift." Sighing, she laid her head against his chest. "I don't ever want to get up from here."

"Neither do I, but unfortunately we must. Once Stryder returns with the MacKaids, Reginald will know I ran off with you. It won't take him long to figure out where we're heading. We needs beat his men to the harbor and be gone before they stop us again."

Cat ground her teeth in frustration. "Can't we ever have a moment to ourselves?"

He toyed with her hair between his fingers. "You're a princess on the run from your father. Unfortunately, lass, such a thing will never allow you rest."

It was true. But that didn't mean she had to like it. "Very well." Sighing, she pushed herself up and began righting her clothes.

Lochlan watched as she tucked herself back into her gown. He hated that they lacked the leisure of spending the night together completely naked. She'd deserved more than a quick tumble for her first time.

And as he fastened his pants, a fear raked him. "If there should be a babe—"

She placed her hand over his lips to silence his words. "I know, Lochlan. But let's not taint this moment with that fear. If it should come to pass, we will deal with it together. There are far worse things in life than being bastard born."

And she would know, having been such herself. Even so, her strength amazed him. There weren't many women who felt that way. "I will keep you safe, Catarina. Always."

"I know and I shall endeavor to keep myself from harm so as not to cause you damage."

Laughing, he pulled her against him so that he could kiss her. He kept her lips between his tongue and his teeth as he pulled back.

Cat trembled as she realized a hard truth about their relationship.

She loved him.

Part of her wanted to blurt it out, but the other was afraid of what he'd say. Not to mention the fact that they had no hope of a relationship. She couldn't marry without her father's approval and he would never allow an alliance between her and a simple Scottish laird.

He'd kill Lochlan in an instant and the Lord only knew what he'd do to Lochlan's people and family.

Nay. Tonight was all they would ever have and she would have to content herself with it.

Her heart heavy, she watched as he pulled his tunic over his head and laced it. As she started to mount her horse, Lochlan stopped her.

"Ride with me and you can sleep while we journey."

And he would be holding her. That alone made her nod as she moved toward him. He swung her up on his horse before he took the reins of her mare and tied them to his saddle.

She let out a shaky breath as he swung himself up behind her. His arms surrounded her body. Smiling, she leaned back against his chest so that she could stare up at him.

For once his stern features were relaxed and it made her smile all the more. There was nothing more incredible than the feel of him against her.

Impulsively, she lifted her head so that she could nip at the stubble on his chin.

He hissed at her actions. "You keep doing that, lass, and we'll never make it to the port before Reginald's men overtake us."

Laughing, she wrapped her arm around his neck. "It might be worth it."

His eyes seared her. "You would be worth a beating or two I think."

Her heart warm, Cat closed her eyes and just enjoyed the sensation of being in his arms. All her life she'd wondered what it would be like to feel this way about a man. Now she knew. It was frightening and wonderful.

If only it could last. She wanted to ask him to run away with her, but she knew the answer.

He had a clan and a family. People who relied on him. He'd never give those up for anything. Not even her.

But here in the night, she let her imagination free so that she could see them together in her mind. See their children playing while they watched.

Lochlan leaned his cheek against the top of her head as her breath stirred against his chest. How he wished they could stay together. If only Catarina wasn't a princess whose father was bent on using her for political advantage. While his clan was large and strong, it wouldn't hold any type of appeal for a French king. Too much land separated their borders.

And he wasn't one of his brothers who could leave the MacAllister lands to settle here in France. His people and family all depended on him. No doubt there would be crisis aplenty for him to deal with on his return.

But here for a moment he could pretend that he was just a man and Catarina only a woman. That the two of them could have a future together. Tonight there was no one else on this earth, save the two of them.

She was his and he was hers.

Yet how he dreaded the morrow. Most of all he dreaded the day he was going to have to watch her walk out of his life.

God help me be strong. Because he knew the truth. He would crawl on his knees to keep her.

Terrified of that knowledge, he cupped her head in his hand and placed a tender kiss to her hair. He felt her lips curl into a smile as she relaxed even more.

In no time at all, she was asleep. Strangely, it seemed as if he'd known her forever. It was hard to believe just how much she'd come to mean to him in such a short time.

Yet there was no denying what he felt in his heart. She'd touched him in a way no one ever had. He would never be the same again.

For that he could almost hate her. But there was no hate inside him now. Only a quiet peace. He didn't understand how she could simultaneously excite and calm him.

Doing his best not to think about that and what it signified, he guided his horse through the darkness for the next few hours.

Dawn was just about to break as they entered Honfleur. He was surprised to see a few people actually about . . . most of them winding their way home after a night of carousing. Though to be fair, there were a few shopkeepers at work as well. One of them gave him a friendly nod as he came outside to sweep the area before his store.

His eyes heavy, Lochlan had to force himself not to sleep. There had to be an inn around here where they could rest for a bit.

That was the thought foremost on his mind as he turned down a small side street that led to the docks. As they neared one particularly large ship, he realized that it must have just come into port. The crew was shouting as they lowered anchors and secured it.

He didn't think anything about it until he looked up to see its colors.

His heart stopped beating as he recognized them.

'Twas the personal banner for Philip Capet, King of France, father of Catarina.

And said man was looking right at him.

Chapter 13

The sanest move would most likely be to spur the horse around and run as swiftly as possible away from the man who would demand his head if he recognized Catarina. But Lochlan didn't. For one thing, he wasn't sure if the king could recognize the woman in his arms while she slept with her face turned into his chest or not.

And if Lochlan were to run, it would definitely alert them that he was afraid of being seen. No doubt they'd pursue out of curiosity and discover Catarina.

That would certainly be his death.

Therefore, the safest course of action was to continue his slow journey to the inn at the end of the street and pray that wasn't the king's destination as well. Otherwise, it was going to be a most miserable, if not short, night.

Act nonchalant. Act uninterested. For God's sake, don't get twitchy.

Well, it would help if he didn't feel as if every man on that ship was watching him with intent.

They're not. Stay focused.

That was a hard thing to do when the outcome of this could very well be a painful death for him. His heart pounding, Lochlan inclined his head to a sailor who was mooring the ship. He kept his gaze straight, forcing himself not to look up at the king, who was now speaking to a man by his side.

"Halt!"

Lochlan had to force himself to rein his horse and not kick it forward. He glanced down to make sure Catarina's face was covered by the sleeve of his tunic before he turned around in the saddle to see one of the king's men approaching him. "Aye?"

"Are you local?"

Lochlan hesitated as he wondered why the man would ask him that. "Afraid not."

The nobleman cursed. "Is there any chance you'll know where we might find a Lord Mortimer?"

Grateful he wasn't seeking a Lord Lochlan or an executioner, Lochlan shook his head. "Nay, my lord. I've no idea."

The man's gaze dropped down to Catarina before he apologized. "Forgive me. I didn't realize you had your wife with you."

Lochlan smiled to cover his relief that the knight couldn't see more of her. "'Tis nothing to worry over. She sleeps very soundly."

Thank the Lord and all His saints for that. Otherwise, she'd be waking and exposing them both to the executioner's noose.

The nobleman inclined his head. "Good morning to you, my lord."

"And to you."

Lochlan nudged his horse forward even though his stomach was tight enough to form a diamond. Every step of the hoof made him anticipate another cry from the king or his men.

It wasn't until he reached the inn that he was able to draw a real breath again. From here they should be safe. He glanced back to the ship to see them unloading horses.

Whispering a prayer of gratitude, he held Catarina tight against him and slid to the ground. He kept her carefully shielded while he knocked on the door and waited for the keeper to admit them.

A small, wiry old man opened the door to peer up at him. "Aye?"

"Have you a room to let, good sir?"

Scratching his cheek, he nodded and opened the door wider. "There's a room for you, my lord. Do you be needing a hand with your horses?"

"Aye, please."

"I'll see to them as soon as you and your lady are settled."

Lochlan entered and noted that the place was small, but clean and well kept. "My thanks."

The man inclined his head before he closed the door and led Lochlan to a room on the first floor, about midway down a long, narrow hallway.

The inn was completely silent, which was good. Only the innkeeper had seen them, so no one could mention his appearance to one of the king's men should they happen upon them or the king. The fewer who knew about Catarina's presence, the better.

"My name is Reynard." He opened the door to the room and stood back so that Lochlan could carry Catarina to the bed and lay her down. "If you be needing anything, don't hesitate to ask. I'll be at my post by the door until my brother, Rolfe, awakens. He'll be just as happy to help you, my lord. I'll be putting your horses in our stable in back. There's good oats for them and fresh water."

"Thank you, Reynard." Lochlan handed him a coin and made sure to tip him well.

His face lightened instantly. "My pleasure to serve you, my lord. Remember, anything you need . . . anything at all."

It wasn't until Reynard was gone that Lochlan realized that the innkeeper hadn't asked for his name. Then again, this close to the docks, he was probably used to men who used aliases anyway. It was probably better for him not to know the identity of who he housed here.

Grateful for that, Lochlan pulled his sword off and balanced it on the table by the bed. It wasn't until he went to remove his boots that it dawned on him he'd had them on the entire time he'd made love to Catarina.

For that alone, he felt terrible. They'd been so incredibly rushed, and she hadn't even complained. She deserved so much better than what he'd given her.

Jerking his boots off, he tossed them to the floor before he turned around to remove her small, delicate shoes. The sight of the rope burns around her ankles angered him even more. He should have killed Graham for what he'd done to her. Bastard.

But at least she was safe now and he had no intention of letting her out of his sight—

Until she demanded it. Lochlan cursed at the knowledge. He'd promised to free her as soon as they found her uncle. And he would abide by that even if it killed him.

You've suffered worse.

He flinched as he saw the memory of his father in bed with Maire in his mind.

The bastard hadn't even had the decency to apologize for it. *She's just another whore. What care you who crawls inside her? If not me, 'twould have been one of your brothers.*

But Catarina would never do something like that. She wouldn't crawl into another man's bed.

Grateful for that fact, he gathered her in his arms and held her close as he allowed his exhaustion to overtake him.

Cat sighed as she came awake to the sensation of a warm body pressing up against her. Even without looking, she knew the feel of those steely arms.

She smiled as she realized Lochlan must have found them a safe, comfortable place to sleep.

Opening her eyes, she saw a small, slightly parted window. The sound of the sea and of people talking and moving about filled her ears. They must have made it to town and Lochlan had once again brought her inside and tucked her into bed without waking her.

He was so thoughtful that way.

"I hope to heaven she runs before we get there."

Cat froze at the Romanian words. More than that, she knew the voice speaking them.

Viktor!

Her heart thrumming in excitement, she launched herself from the bed to draw closer to the window. Had she misheard? Was it even possible . . .

"Aye, it'll be bad for her if she's there when we arrive."

And Bavel, too! Tears pricked her eyes as she heard their voices. Carefully, she cracked open the window to make sure no one else was with them. Once she was certain it was clear, she gave a low whistle.

Viktor was the first to turn in her direction.

Tall and dark, he was as handsome as any man could be. And the instant his black gaze focused on her location, his entire face lit up. He popped Bavel in the chest before he rushed to her window. "Wild Catarina, thank the Lord that you're all right."

She put her hand outside the window so that she could touch him. It was so good to feel his touch again. "Oh Viktor, Bavel, I've missed you two more than I can even begin to relay. I can't believe you're here."

Bavel pushed her back inside and closed the window to nothing more than a bare crack. "We're not alone, kitten. Your father's with us."

Her joy ended instantly. "What?"

Bavel glanced about nervously before he answered. "He knew you'd be looking for us, so we're in his custody. He hopes you'll find us and he can snatch you away again. Any moment now one of his men is sure to come seeking us. We're not to stray far from them."

"A pox on that man!" she snarled.

Ignoring her outburst, Viktor stepped closer. "We had word you were in Rouen and that's where we're headed."

"I was until last night." She glanced over her shoulder to where Lochlan continued to sleep. "I'm very safe at present. I'm traveling with Lochlan MacAllister."

Viktor gaped.

"The stiff Scot prig?"

She blushed at Bavel's indignant question.

Viktor scoffed. "Be grateful for that. At least we know he won't harm or touch her."

Bavel nodded. "Aye, that's true. He's much preferable to some of those brothers of his."

"Listen," she said quickly as she caught sight of men nearing them. "I'm traveling with Lochlan to England to meet his brother. Can you get free of my father's men?"

Bavel shook his head. "Not likely, but we can try."

She stepped back even farther so that no one outside would be able to see her. "If you don't find me there, then meet in Scotland. I'll be with Lochlan until you come for me."

Bavel stepped back and turned around so that it would appear he was talking to Viktor. "Love to you, kitten. God keep you safe."

She sniffed back her tears at the love she heard in his voice. "Same to you, Uncle. Now go before we all get into trouble."

She'd barely shut the window before two guards found them.

"What are you doing?" the guard demanded in a fierce, angry tone.

"We got a bit lost," Bavel said good-naturedly. "These French towns all look alike."

The guard scoffed.

"Are we going back to the Sailor's Inn?" Viktor asked.

"Until the king finishes his food and is ready to depart, aye."

Cat blessed her family for being so smart in letting her know their plans and where her father was located. Now it would be easier to avoid her father until they could leave. Grateful to them, she went back to bed only to find Lochlan giving her a peeved glare.

"What?"

"Stiff prig am I?" he asked in an offended tone.

She cocked a brow at him. "Would you rather I tell them exactly how unpriggish you are and why it is I know it?"

He rolled over to give her his back. "You still could have defended me."

Was he serious? Of course he was. There was no way he was feigning this amount of petulance.

Cat tsked at him before she reached under the covers to draw small circles on his back. "Poor Lochlan. Everyone insults my baby."

He didn't speak.

Nipping at his shoulder, she ran her hand around him to find out that he was indeed *very* stiff. He grabbed her hand as if to pull it away, but before he could, she brushed the tip of his cock with her nails.

He let out a deep groan before he pressed her hand closer to him.

She rolled him onto his back. "Feeling better?"

"Nay."

She continued to stroke him. "Not even a little?"

"Perhaps. You keep doing that, lass, and I might go straight past better and into ecstasy."

She laughed before she dipped her head to suckle his nipple lightly.

Lochlan sucked his breath in sharply as he reached to unlace her gown. A part of him argued they should be finding a ship for England, but the other part said the safest place was right here. So long as her father was in town, either he or one of his men could find them. Besides, they would have to wait for Stryder and his group to return.

What better way to wait than this?

Pulling back, he quickly divested her of her gown. He growled in appreciation as he saw her beauty for the first time. Truly no woman had ever been more beautiful. He nipped playfully at her breast before he quickly undressed himself. Completely naked, he pulled her against him and savored the sensation of her skin touching his.

In that one moment, he wished that time could stop. That this was all there was to his life. He could live and die happily if all there was in the world was waking in her arms and going to sleep every night with the touch of her hand on his face.

This was perfection.

Cat closed her eyes and breathed Lochlan in as they kissed. This was the closest to heaven she would ever come without dying and she didn't want it to end.

He rolled her over, placing her on top of him. She lifted herself up so that she could stare down at his playful blue eyes. He cupped her face in his hands and stroked her lips with the pads of his thumbs. God, he was handsome and strong.

She returned his smile before she took his right hand and brought it to her lips so that she could lightly tease the pads of his fingers. She loved how his hands felt in hers. Most of all, she loved how they felt on her body.

Lochlan was torn between playing with her at his leisure and being inside her. He didn't know what it was about her, but she soothed him on a level unimaginable. She also set fire to his soul.

His impatience winning, he lifted her up and set her down on top of him.

They groaned in unison as she took him in all the way to his hilt. He ground his teeth as she moved excruciatingly slow against him. Her strokes were sweet and hesitant from her inexperience. He watched her as he moved his hand to touch her stomach. Even though he had no right to the thought, he imagined what it would be like to watch her grow round with his child. To be by her side while she brought a babe into this world.

She would make a fierce mother, who would give him strong, confident sons . . . and daughters.

He smiled at the thought.

Cat frowned at the tender expression on Lochlan's face. "What are thinking of?"

"You, my love. Only you."

"And that makes you smile?"

"Always."

Warmth consumed her. "I can't believe I ever thought you priggish."

"I can't believe I ever thought you annoying."

She stopped and grimaced at him. "You're an awful monster."

"And you are the most beautiful blossom I've ever been fortunate enough to find."

His compliment made her blush. "You're such a cad."

"As you wish."

She arched a surprised brow at him. "You're not arguing with me?"

"While I'm inside you? Nay. Honestly, I don't even know what either one of us is saying. I really don't care. My thoughts are only consumed by how good you look naked and much I love being inside you."

She tsked at him. "Then you'll regret later that you just promised me the leadership of your clan."

"Mmm. Whatever makes you happy."

Cat laughed. Truthfully, what made her happiest was the sensation of being in his arms. Of having his hard body against hers. She loved this man and this really was all she wanted in her life.

If only she could have it.

Closing her eyes, she savored every thrust of him against her. Every stroke she delivered to him. And when she came, he joined her instantly.

Hot and sweating, she collapsed against him while he gathered her in his arms and held her to his chest like a precious bundle.

Neither of them moved for ever so long. It wasn't until hunger overcame them that Lochlan got up and dressed and went to seek food for them while Cat took her time washing and dressing.

They spent the rest of the day hidden, waiting for word from the others. As the hours passed with no communication or word, Lochlan began to get concerned. Stryder would have had more than enough time to return to Rouen and travel back to the docks.

Where could he be?

As the sun set, he left Catarina hidden in the room and went to look for them. The king's ship was still moored where it'd been last night. Only now there was no activity except for two lone guards who watched over it.

Ignoring them, Lochlan continued on, scanning the street for any sign of the others. There were sailors aplenty, a few prostitutes soliciting clients, and merchants negotiating deals and rushing to and fro.

His worst fear was that Stryder and group were now in royal custody for their parts in planning his escape. It would make sense. They'd helped him free Catarina and Lochlan was sure Graham would gladly relate the events to Reginald and his men.

"Lochlan."

He paused at the whispered shout. It took him several seconds before he located the source of it.

Dressed all in black with even a cowl to cover his head, Kestrel stood in the shadow of a building. He motioned Lochlan over to him.

As soon as he joined him, Kestrel pulled him deeper into the alleyway.

Lochlan ground his teeth as anger and fear assailed him. "Have the others been taken?"

"In a manner of speaking. Aye."

He scowled at the odd note in Kestrel's voice. "What do you mean?"

"The king spotted us as we came into town and demanded Stryder spend a few moments with him. Those moments have turned into all damn day."

Lochlan let out a sound of disgust. "But Stryder's not under arrest?"

He shook his head. "Trust me. We put the fear of God into Graham and his brothers. He speaks one word against us and he'll be begging for death before he finishes the first syllable."

That made him feel a little better. "So we wait on Stryder?"

"Nay. The king could very well be watching him since he's the English king's champion. Stryder said for us to go ahead and he'd catch up to us. He thinks it best that he keep the king distracted while we make our getaway."

"And if he fails and is caught?"

"Don't worry. He won't. Stryder is smarter than that."

"What about my brother? Stryder said that he'd—"

"Again, don't worry," Kestrel said, cutting him off. "The Scot knows me and he'll let us enter even without Stryder." He indicated a small boat that was loading cargo. "They sail within the hour. I've already arranged passage for all of us. Retrieve Catarina and hide belowdeck until it's safe."

"What about you?"

"I'll be there, but since the king has already seen me with Stryder, I don't want to draw his attention to you."

The man was extremely paranoid. However, given their situation and the repercussions that could fall on all their heads, it was probably a good thing.

Lochlan nodded. "I'll see you on board."

Kestrel drifted back into the shadows and actually seemed to have disappeared. Lochlan crossed himself. There were times when that man seemed to possess demonic powers.

Putting that out of his mind, he went back to the inn to collect Catarina.

He found her waiting by the window, picking at a loaf of bread. She let out a relieved breath the instant she saw him. "I was beginning to get worried."

"There was nothing to worry over. We only have a king who wants you captive and me dead . . . one who's staying at the end of this street, talking to Stryder and Simon. How could that cause anyone concern?"

"I see your point," she said, feigning relief. "How utterly foolish of me to be concerned."

Lochlan shook his head at her retort. "Stryder will catch up to us. We have a ship waiting to take us to England. As soon as you're—"

She stood immediately. "I'm more than ready to put as much distance as possible between my father and me. Let us run for that boat."

His heart clenched at her words. How awful to feel that way about the man who'd sired her, but then he'd felt no better about his own. It was a shame that the world was filled with such people.

He picked up her cloak and wrapped it around her before he lifted the cowl to conceal her face. As he did so he was struck by the irony of a woman so vivacious wanting to be invisible. She deserved a man who could appreciate her unique qualities. One who wouldn't try to stifle her.

Closing his eyes, he kissed her on the top of her head. She took his hand in hers and that small gesture brought him to his knees. He squeezed her hand before he led her from the room.

He paused downstairs to settle his account before he took her outside to the docks. It was darker now, with storm clouds brewing. He didn't see any sign of Kestrel as they made their way toward the boat Kestrel had indicated.

Lochlan allowed her to mount the gangplank first. He scanned the docks one last time before he followed her up.

A small, heavyset sailor approached them. "You the Scot's man?"

"Aye."

"His lordship told me to put you below." He showed them to a cramped room that held four chairs and a short table. "Stay here and we'll be sailing very soon."

"My thanks."

The man nodded before he left them alone.

Cat let out a slow breath as she lowered her

cowl. Even so, she knew better than to count on their safety just yet. She wouldn't feel completely relieved until France was out of her sight.

Suddenly, she heard the sound of someone running down the hallway outside. They were headed for her room.

Lochlan pulled his sword from its sheath an instant before the door was slammed open.

Kestrel was there, his cheeks red from his run. "The king is coming. We have to hide the two of you immediately."

Chapter 14

"How is that possible?" Lochlan asked.

Kestrel gave him a droll stare. "I don't know. Now we can either hide you or keep arguing until you're both taken into custody. Your choice."

Cat growled at the man's sarcasm. Any other time, she might have had an appreciation for it. In this moment, however, she could have done without it. "Hide us where?"

Kestrel bolted the door behind him before he indicated a group of barrels against the back wall.

Cat glanced at them skeptically. Nice thought, but unless they had enough time to empty the barrels, which would leave a most obvious clue as to where they were hiding, it was a useless one. "Those are full."

"Really?" he asked, his face a mask of mockery, "I wasn't planning on putting you in one. Stand on top of it and crawl up there." He pointed to the ceiling.

Now that was even more ridiculous than hiding them in the barrels. "They'll find us there."

"Trust me. No one ever looks up. No one. Even as low as this ceiling is, it'll never occur to them to seek you there."

Lochlan looked as skeptical as she felt. "Are you willing to bet your life on it?"

"Nay," Kestrel said with a smile, "but I'm willing to bet yours."

Cat was sure the unamused look on her face matched the one on Lochlan's.

Lochlan glanced up at the ceiling, then narrowed his gaze on Kestrel. "If they find us, you're the first one I kill."

"Please. Better to die quickly by your hand than be tortured again."

Before Cat could ask about that phrase, Kestrel had them climb up the barrels to the ceiling. There was a small ledge that barely accommodated her. Poor Lochlan was left hanging by the strength of his arms and legs. She wasn't even sure how he managed it. No doubt it was painful. But he didn't say a word about it.

Satisfied with their positions, Kestrel threw netting around them, tucking it around their bodies before he nodded. He stepped down to peer up at them. "You don't make a sound and they'll never know."

Before she could blink, he was out the door.

Still not completely sold on this plan, she glanced to Lochlan. "This isn't very comfortable, now is it?" she said, trying not to speak too loudly.

"I can think of better times I've had."

She smiled at his unexpected humor given the danger they were in.

At least until she heard voices outside. But it wasn't until she heard her father's that she started to panic. This was a foolish place to hide. They were practically in plain sight.

Just as she was about to try and run, Lochlan took her hand in his. The steely blue eyes bolstered her courage immediately. "Trust in Kestrel, lass."

She wasn't sure why Lochlan trusted him, but as the voices drew closer, she realized she didn't have any choice except to see this through.

She heard her father growl. "I swear that girl is

half witch like her mother. I've never seen anyone vanish into thin air before."

"Well, sire, the informant swore that she would be heading out this night on a boat for England. And this is the most likely boat for her to take."

"Are you sure we can trust your informant?"

"Aye, sire. He heard them planning their escape."

"Who else was in the planning?"

"Lords Stryder of Blackmoor and Simon of Anwyk."

Her father cursed. "Two men I can't touch or intimidate and there they both sat across from me, looking me in the eye and not telling me of this. Damn them to hell."

The door rattled on its hinges.

Cat held her breath as it was thrown open and a group of four guards came inside to search. She tightened her grip on Lochlan's hand. This was it, she was sure of it. Any second they'd look up at see them.

Closing her eyes, she prayed furiously.

Below her, the guards overturned the barrels, threw crates aside, and looked everywhere for them.

Except up.

She truly couldn't believe it as they finished their search, then filed one by one out of the room.

"'Tis empty, Your Majesty."

Her father cursed in the hallway before they moved to the next room down.

Cat let out a nervous laugh.

Lochlan motioned her to continue her silence. "We're not out of this until they're gone and we've sailed," he whispered.

She nodded. He was right, but she still felt the need to scream out in relief that Kestrel's trick had worked. Oh if the man were here, she'd kiss him for it.

They continued their uncomfortable perches until her legs had gone numb. It'd been a while since she'd last heard her father's voice. Even so, they didn't want to take the chance on being discovered when they were this close to being gone.

Suddenly, she could feel the ship pulling away from the dock before the door opened again.

It wasn't Kestrel.

Her heart stopped at the sight of a stranger in their haven. He appeared to be an older sailor who walked with a pronounced limp. He hobbled his way toward them before he righted several of the barrels. Then, he looked up at them and grinned.

"Next time I tell you something, you'll be listening to me, eh?"

She was aghast at the disguise. "Kestrel?"

He winked at her before he stood up on the barrel to cut her down. "And now you know how I came by my name. I used to hide in the trees like a bird until it was safe for me to take flight."

She laughed out loud. "And grateful for that are we. Thank you."

"Anytime, my lady." He helped her down before he moved to cut the netting from Lochlan.

"Is the king gone?" he asked as he lowered himself to the floor.

Kestrel nodded. "They weren't happy either. I pity whatever informant they had. I'm sure the man will pay well for that loose tongue. If it wasn't for the fact it would have ended our lives"—he indicated himself and Lochlan—"had we been caught, I'd feel sorry for him. As it is, I hope they cut out his tongue and hang the bastard."

Cat wished she were more charitable, but honestly, she couldn't agree more. Whoever it was, they'd never done anything to him to warrant such hostility. So why that person would try to ruin their lives for nothing more than pure meanness made no sense to her whatsoever. Her mother had always said such treachery only harmed the one carrying it. And she was right.

So like Kestrel, she hoped they hanged the man.

Lochlan straightened up the netting before he addressed Kestrel. "Did Stryder and Simon make it?"

"The sailing? Nay. But they won't be far behind us and Bracken and his family are in the care of Simon's wife. All should be well."

She let out a relieved breath. "Good. I would never want someone hurt because of me."

Kestrel snorted. "And I concur most whole-heartedly. I would never want to be hurt because of you either."

Cat laughed. Kestrel had an infectious sense of humor at times.

"By the way, your uncle bade me pass this note on to you." He pulled a small piece of folded vellum from his pocket and handed it to her.

Cat unfolded it to read what Bavel had to say.

I'm so glad we had the chance to see you, kitten. You've no idea how much we've missed your presence. Viktor can't cook at all. Why does he think well-done means charred? Or that brushing the dirt off is the same as cleaning?

She laughed at a truth she knew well.

But seriously, one word to you, kitten. Your father does love you, but he doesn't see you. He has an ideal of you and though you are ideal, you're not the woman he thinks of. Stay hidden for us. I couldn't bear the thought of your being trapped with these people. You would never survive it. Stay safe and we will meet you soon.

Tears welled in her eyes. And she didn't miss the fact that he'd been careful not to mention where she and Lochlan were going or the fact that Lochlan was with her. Bavel was ever quick that way.

"Is everything all right?" Lochlan asked in a concerned tone.

"Aye. I just miss him terribly."

Lochlan gave her a tender smile before he looked at Kestrel. "How long to England?"

"We'll be in Portsmouth in a couple of hours. Then it's two to three hours more to reach the Scot's home. We could be there by midnight."

Cat was delighted for Lochlan. But as she met his gaze, she saw his reservation. They could journey all this way only to find out a truth he might not want to hear.

"Would we be better to wait until morning?"

she asked Kestrel. "I would hate to disturb his household in the middle of the night."

Kestrel shook his head. "Many of the Brotherhood are nocturnal. They prefer to sleep in the day and stay up all night."

That made little sense to her. "Why?"

Lochlan let out a long breath before he answered. "Because people . . . and bad memories attack best at night. It's when someone is most vulnerable."

Kestrel nodded.

Lochlan met Kestrel's gaze and gave him a subtle tilt of his head to let him know that he understood why the man slept with a lit candle near and a dagger in his hand. He'd been there himself more times than he wanted to remember.

To Catarina's credit she appeared to understand that as well.

"Should we go topside?" she asked.

Kestrel shook his head. "Call me restless and worried, but I think it best we wait here. Once the ship docks, I'll go get horses and come back for you. I think the fewer people who see us, the better."

"I hate it myself," she agreed. "But understand."

So the three of them made themselves comfortable for the trip ahead. Kestrel by perching on top of a barrel so that he could see out a slit in the side of the ship and she by leaning against Lochlan's side while they sat on the floor.

There was something unbelievably soothing about being this close to Lochlan while the ship rolled beneath her. Never in her life had she felt so safe. His presence soothed her even though her life had been torn apart and she was running from a future that would like as not catch up to her.

Amazed by the peace she felt, she took his hand into hers. "Have you thought about what you'll say to your brother?"

"Aye. *Hello* seems like a good start."

She laughed. "I'm serious, Lochlan."

"As am I." His eyes twinkled before they turned deadly earnest. "It depends on if he's Kieran or another. I fear if it's Kieran I may choke the life from him before either of us speaks over what he's put our family through."

She tsked at him and his groundless threat. "I know you better than that. Most likely you will embrace him and welcome him back."

He scoffed a bit. "Aye, but the urge to strangle will be great."

"But you will restrain yourself."

He picked her hand up from his arm to toy idly

with her fingers. The sensation of his touch on her skin made chills spread throughout her body.

"You have much faith in me, lass."

She wrinkled her nose at him before she responded. "I do and I know you, prig that you are."

Lochlan shook his head at her and her teasing. If anyone else had said that to him, he'd have been highly offended. But from her, those insults seemed more like endearments.

There was something very wrong with him.

And then his thoughts turned to Kieran. His stomach was drawn tight in reservation and yet her presence comforted him. So long as she was with him, he believed everything would turn out justly. It was the only time in his life he'd felt this way.

Catarina was a treasure.

He glanced over his head to see Kestrel. "Could you give us a moment?"

Kestrel didn't move for a second. It was as if it took him a moment to realize someone had spoken to him. "Aye." And before Lochlan could blink, he was out of the room.

Lochlan was taken aback by his actions. "That man moves entirely too fast."

Catarina nodded. "He is unearthly at times."

But that wasn't what Lochlan wanted to discuss. He had most serious matters to speak of. Taking Catarina's hands into his, he held them tight and turned toward her. The curiosity in those dark eyes seared him and for a heartbeat his courage faltered.

However, the heat of her hands on his brought it back tenfold and that allowed his tongue to work again. "I want to be with you, Catarina."

She frowned at him. "You are with me."

"Nay . . . 'tis not what I mean, lass." He swallowed before he forced himself to say to her exactly what he meant. "I want to take you to wife."

Cat couldn't breathe as she heard the words she'd never dreamed he'd speak. Part of her still wasn't sure she wasn't dreaming or mistaken.

Lochlan MacAllister wanted to marry her?

It was inconceivable and yet it was a dream come true. But she understood the sacrifice such a thing would require. Did he? "Lochlan . . . I . . . do you understand what you're asking?"

His gaze burned into hers with the passion of his conviction. "More than anything."

She still wasn't so certain. "Do you know what my father will do if he learns of this?"

"I don't care."

Tears welled in her eyes. "Your clan—"

"My brother can take it. Braden would make a . . ." He hesitated as if reconsidering what he was about to say. ". . . decent laird."

She laughed, refusing to believe he would actually abandon his people for her. "My father will never stop hunting us, Lochlan. He has promised me to another and he doesn't take defeat well."

Lochlan scoffed at her fears. "And neither does a Scot. Remember, we are the only country Rome couldn't tame. They had put a wall up to protect themselves from us."

She laughed at the reminder of Hadrian's Wall, which had indeed been built for that very reason.

"If you will have me, Catarina, I can't promise you how much time we'll have together, but I can promise you that whether it's only this one hour or a million more, I will love you for every one of them."

She let out a small sob at words that cut through her heart and made it ache. No man had ever said such to her and no one had ever spoken with such sincerity. She threw herself against him and held him close as her emotions choked and drowned her. She couldn't speak for the tidal waves that assailed her. All she could do was feel how much she loved him. How much she wanted to spend the rest of her life with this man.

"Catarina?"

She heard the hesitancy in his voice. "I want to be with you, Lochlan," she breathed, her voice breaking. "I do, but I can't if it means your life." She pulled back to look up at him. "And I know for a fact that it would. I'm not selfless enough to be content with a single hour. I'm a greedy woman and I want you with me always."

"Then we will run."

She shook her head. "It's not in you and we both know that. You're not a coward, Lochlan MacAllister. I've seen you stand firm and proud when another man would have begged for mercy. You are what you are and that is why I love you. I don't want you to become something you're not to please me. Neither of us would ever be happy with that." She wanted to say that it was enough for her that he was willing to run.

The truth was very different. It wasn't enough. She wanted to be with him and she was angry that they couldn't be together. It wasn't fair or right.

Lochlan placed a tender kiss to the top of her head and held her close to his heart. Closing his eyes, he expected to hear his father's voice in his head berating him. But there was only silence. How strange that it was only Catarina who could squelch the violence and insults of his past.

She was his peace.

There was a quiet knock before Kestrel opened the door and entered the room. "They're starting to stare at me in the hallway. Sorry."

Catarina pulled away as Kestrel returned to his perch.

There was an awkward silence between them. Cat wanted to speak, but didn't want to voice her concerns before a stranger.

Time passed slowly until Kestrel finally spoke. "By the way"—he paused to turn his head in their direction—"I know 'tis none of my business. But it seems to me that people usually regret the things they don't do more than the things they indeed do."

He returned to stare out at the sea with an expression of heartache so profound that she could feel it within her own chest. "I had a lady once who I loved more than my own life who begged me to stay with her and not go to Outremer." He let out a tired breath. "I didn't listen to her pleas. I wanted to go to make money and earn lands for us so that I could treat her like the queen she was in my eyes. But I was gone so long that she assumed me dead and married another."

His face sad, he fell silent before he spoke again. "And every moment of my life, I regret that I didn't stay with her that final day when she begged me to. I didn't think we stood a chance, what with the obstacles we faced and by trying alone to make a future for us, I ensured that we'd never have one at all."

Kestrel turned to give them both a harsh stare of warning. "I guess Stryder is right. We are all damned or saved by the decisions we make. Just don't let fear make the decision for you. There were two things I learned while in hell. One, it's much easier to face the devil and fight when you're not alone. And two, what you envision in the darkness of your mind is always much more frightening than the realities that come at you. The devil always blinks first. Stand your ground and fear nothing."

Cat wiped at the single tear that fell from her eye at his words and the pain they betrayed, which he hid so carefully. Yet for their future, he was willing to bare his scars to them. It said much for the man and she pitied the woman who had haplessly let him go. "Thank you, Kestrel."

He inclined his head to her. "I don't want to see

someone else make my mistake. If you're both willing to run, then run until they find you and don't look back. Ever. Believe me, the world is large and there are places you can live where no one will ever find you again."

Lochlan paused as he thought about Kieran and all the years his brother had been missing. Kestrel was right. His brother had run and none of them had ever known his whereabouts. Not in all this time.

Perhaps they could have a future after all.

He held his hand up for Catarina. "Will you run with me, Cat?"

The hesitation in her eyes brought a wave of fear to him. If she rejected him again, he wasn't sure what he'd do.

She glanced to Kestrel before she nodded. "To the ends of this earth, I will run with you, Lochlan MacAllister."

Chapter 15

For the first time in Lochlan's life, he actually looked forward to the future. For once, he had one worth living for.

As soon as they tied up this last mystery with his brother, he and Catarina would begin their life together. Neither of them knew where they would go, but it didn't matter.

She was used to earning her living and making do, and she would teach him whatever he needed to know. Not to mention he could earn extra coin at tournament. No one had ever bested him in a joust and few could defeat him at sword. They would be fine, he was sure of it.

He waited on the docks with Catarina while Kestrel bought them new mounts that would take them to the Scot's castle. This late at night, there were very few people about. But even so, he was careful. They still didn't know who Philip's informer had been.

But even with that weight on him, he still felt freer than he'd ever been before.

Kestrel returned with the horses. Lochlan smiled in approval. The man had chosen healthy, fast mounts for them.

"My thanks."

Kestrel gave him a wry smile. "I hope they never come in handy."

Lochlan laughed as he swung Catarina up into her saddle. "That makes two of us." Running from a king's justice was never good and often made bloody bedfellows.

Mounting his own horse, he allowed Kestrel to take the lead.

They rode in silence with nothing more than the bright moonlight as company. The sound of wolves echoed in the distance. There was a light mist on the ground, but even so there was nothing ominous about the night.

At least not until they reached the Scot's castle. It sat up on top of a high hill with a road so narrow, they were forced to ride single file. More than that, it was so narrow that even the horses were nervous and had to move very slowly lest they lose their footing.

"We should have dismounted," Catarina said from behind them.

"Too late now," they said in unison. There was no way to dismount without falling down the side of the hill and most likely dying painfully on the sharp rocks below.

The Scot had planned this location well. No one would ever be able to take his fortress. Nor would they be able to approach it without being seen. Something that became obvious as they reached the small clearing before the castle's opening.

Kestrel reined his horse and made sure he was within the circle of light that fell from the battlements above. It allowed visitors to be seen clearly, while the visitors could tell nothing of those who stood above, watching them.

"Raziel, 'tis the Kestrel. I bring friends in search of the Scot. Let us in."

Lochlan could only see shadowed outlines on the battlements above them. For all he knew they were getting ready to pour oil over all three of them and set them on fire. It was an unnerving thought.

The silence rang out for several minutes.

"Did he hear you?" Lochlan finally asked.

His answer came as one of the doors before them scraped open. There in the doorway was a tall, lean Saracen who was dressed in dark blue and gold-trimmed flowing robes. With an aura of extreme power, he wore two swords crossed over his back. Arms akimbo, he didn't appear pleased by their late-night visit.

"Kestrel," he said, his voice nothing more than a deep rumble. "It's been a long time, old friend."

"Aye. Thanks for not shooting me . . . this time."

Raziel's face showed no sign of amusement. "You will never forget that, will you?"

"I still limp and feel the bite of the wound every time it rains. How could I?" Kestrel dismounted before he joined Raziel and clapped him on the back like a brother.

Grateful the tension was broken, Lochlan dismounted, then moved to help Catarina down.

As they approached the Saracen, Raziel's black eyes narrowed dangerously.

"They're not us," he growled at Kestrel. "Who have you brought here and why?"

"I'm Lochlan MacAllister."

Raziel hissed before he pulled a sword free and angled it at Lochlan's throat. "Are you mad?" he snarled through clenched teeth. "The Scot will lose what little mind he has left."

Lochlan couldn't breathe as anticipation, fear, and trepidation mingled inside him. "He's my brother. I want to see him."

"You abandoned him." The accusation hung heavy in the air, but it wasn't the truth and Lochlan knew it.

"I have never abandoned a brother in my life. Ever. And I won't let that lie stand."

"I believe him," Kestrel said, pushing Raziel's blade to the side with his bare hand. "He's traveled far for the truth. What say we speak to the Scot alone and see what he has to say?"

Raziel snorted. "You'll be lucky if you're not gutted on the floor like a pig. The Scot has no interest in the past."

Still Kestrel argued for them. "Have a heart, Raziel. Lochlan isn't like my family. He's not going to spit on the Scot for surviving. Let us speak to him and see what he has to say."

Raziel curled his lip before he finally sheathed his sword. Even so, the disdain he felt for Lochlan was clearly etched into every part of his demeanor. He narrowed his black eyes before he spoke a low, deadly warning. "If you say anything to hurt my lord, I will have your tongue and your heart."

"I won't hurt my brother."

Raziel glared at him one last time before he turned and led them through the outer bailey.

Catarina took his hand in hers as they walked through what was obviously intended to withstand the Second Coming. Lochlan shook his head at the fortifications. Kieran had never cared for such. Though his brother been a natural fighter with good instincts, Kieran had never really cared about conflict or leading. He'd only wanted to play and chase maids.

It was obvious Lochlan was about to face a very different man than the petulant boy who'd left home.

As they walked, he counted at least twenty knights patrolling the battlements and yard. It said much that the Scot had the money to pay them and it spoke even more to his paranoia that they were about at this time of the night. Obviously, the Scot was ready to fight anyone who threatened the sanctity of his home.

Once they reached the castle, Raziel wouldn't allow them to enter anything more than the foyer. "Wait here and don't move."

"May I at least scratch my ear?" Catarina asked impishly.

Raziel curled his lip at her. "You think this is amusing?"

She shook her head before she answered in a sincere tone. "I never find tragedy amusing. But I do believe you see danger where only safety exists. And you grossly misjudge a good man with no knowledge of his character."

Raziel scoffed at her. "How lucky for you that your life has been so gentle that you trust so easily. May Allah always be so kind to you."

With that spoken, he led Kestrel to the stairs.

Cat didn't move again until the two of them were out of sight. "Well," she said, turning toward Lochlan, "they're not exactly friendly here, are they?"

"Apparently not. God save them from whatever it was that has caused them to be this way."

She nodded. He was right. Their pasts must be horrible indeed to warrant this kind of security.

All of a sudden, a fierce shout rang out from the hallway above them. But it was so muffled by the stone that they couldn't make out the words. Only the displeasure of the man's tone.

"Your brother?" she asked Lochlan.

"I know not, but I would assume so. The saints know the man always had a voice that could carry for leagues."

Cat was beginning to think this had been a wasted effort on their part as the shouting continued without letup. She could only imagine how hard this would have to be on Lochlan to have come this far only to be turned away now that they were so close.

And still the angry shouting continued.

Lochlan met her gaze an instant before he headed toward the stairs.

"Lochlan," she called, but he didn't pause as he continued on his way.

Cat lifted the hem of her gown before she followed after him. He stalked toward the chamber with determined strides that said he wasn't going to leave until he had his audience.

And as they drew closer to the room at the end, the words became audible.

"You can't just send him away," Kestrel snarled. "Not after what he's risked to come to you."

"As if I give a damn what he risks. He wasn't there with us in the bowels of hell. He was off in the Highlands, bedding wenches and making merry while we were being tortured and humiliated. The devil take him to hell where he can roast him for eternity."

Cat expected that to give Lochlan pause. Instead, it seemed to fortify him as he reached the doors and swung them wide.

All sound stopped in the wake of the echoing clatter of wood against stone.

She drew up short as she saw the face . . . or what was left of it of Lochlan's brother. It was all she could do not to flinch. But the greatest tragedy was that one side of it was completely perfect and told the world just how beautiful this man had once been.

The other side was scarred horribly by burns and held a single patch over his eye that was no doubt missing. Her stomach sank at the sight of it. How the man must have suffered . . .

Lochlan finally paused as he came face-to-face with a familiar stranger. His heart pounded as he met the one crystal eye that was the same exact color of his father's . . . and Kieran's. In fact, he saw much of Kieran in the features that remained undamaged by savage cruelty and yet . . .

The truth slammed into him with an iron fist. "You're not my brother."

The Scot let out a feral cry so raw that it actually made the hair on the back of Lochlan's neck stand up. He upturned the table before him, before he drew a sword and lunged.

Lochlan barely had time to draw his own and deflect the fierce blow that would have severed his head.

"Bastard!" the Scot snarled, kicking him back. He came at him, but before he could swing again, Kestrel blocked his way.

The Scot spat at Lochlan, then threw his sword at him.

Lochlan caught it in his hand and lowered it to the floor.

Still the man's eyes accused him of treachery and other things Lochlan could only guess at. "I'm as much a MacAllister as you are."

Lochlan winced as he realized the man before him must be one of his father's numerous bastards. "Then I was wrong and you are my brother. For that I am grateful, but please forgive me for what I said. You're just not the brother I was hoping to apologize to."

That took the fight out of him. The Scot literally slumped against Kestrel an instant before he shoved him away.

He turned to Raziel. "I want him out of my castle. Now. Alive or dead, makes no never mind to me."

"Well it makes a difference to me," Catarina snapped. She approached the Scot with her hands on her hips. She raked a scathing glare over him as if she were taking a small child to task for his rude behavior. "How dare you, sir!"

The Scot looked aghast at her. "Have you lost your sense?"

"Nay," she said, lifting her head with pride, "I have not, but 'tis quite apparent you have."

That fired his one eye even more as a fierce muscle worked angrily in his jaw. "Woman—"

"Man!" she spat back, interrupting him. "I've heard quite enough of your ranting this night. 'Tis only right you should hear some of mine."

Lochlan wasn't sure which of them was most stunned as he exchanged a wide-eyed stare with Kestrel.

Raziel started toward her, but she stopped him dead midstride with a look so cold, Lochlan could feel the burn of it.

She then turned that frigid stare to the Scot. "What happened to you is a tragedy to be sure. And for that I am truly sorry for your loss. No man should suffer so. But you could take a moment out of your selfish life to alleviate someone else's suffering. Just once."

He advanced on her then with a lethal twist of his lips. "You know nothing of suffering. Nothing."

"And there you would be wrong, sir. Most wrong." Her voice held the strength and sincerity of a woman who had been pushed too far to back down.

She stood toe to toe with him without hesitation or fear. Lochlan had never before seen her equal.

And when she spoke again, her voice was laden with the pain of her own past and her words evoked an unrivaled anger inside him. "I know exactly what it's like to be held down and beaten for no reason whatsoever. I've tasted my own blood and have felt my teeth loosened from the blows. If you think for one moment that you are alone in the realm of suffering, then think again. The world is filled with those who ache. If we are lucky, our outsides don't bear the scars that shred our souls. Then again, are *we* the lucky ones?"

She didn't really pause for his answer. "When one looks at you, my lord, they see the marks of your past and they treat you with deference over it. When you look at Lochlan or me, you judge us without knowing the price we've both paid in our pasts. How dare you. Of all people, *you* should know better than to do such a thing."

Lochlan braced himself to intervene should the Scot strike her.

He didn't. Instead he stared at her as if imagining her slow dismemberment.

"You're a cheeky wench."

"And you're a bullish oaf."

His eye blank, the Scot looked at Lochlan and shook his head. "God have mercy on you, man, if this is your woman. You should have let me gut you and save you from her tongue."

Lochlan shrugged. "I'm rather fond of that tongue myself. I find it often holds a lot of truth when it speaks."

The Scot reached out then and placed a gentle hand to Catarina's face. There was a subtle gentling of his gaze. "I'd forgotten how soft a woman's skin could be."

He dropped his hand before he turned to face the fire and ambled over to it.

Lochlan frowned at Kestrel, who shrugged at the same time Raziel came forward to retrieve the Scot's sword.

Suddenly, the Scot's low, thick voice filled the air. "Kieran died so that I could live this life, such as it is." He laughed bitterly, then winced as if it caused him unimaginable pain. "He took the blade meant for me and he died in my arms, coughing up blood and begging me to ask you for your forgiveness."

The Scot braced one hand against the mantel. "He said he wanted you to know that he hadn't meant what he'd said to you the last time you'd spoken. That it was thoughtless and cruel and that he loved you. That he respected you." He paused to let out a tired sigh. "All he wanted that last year we spent in prison was to go home and see the lot of you again. He kept saying over and over again that God would not be so merciless as to let the last words between him and his beloved brothers be so cruel. It was why he didn't kill himself that day at the loch even though he didn't want to live anymore. But he didn't have the courage to face you. He just wanted the pain to end. He didn't want to see the judgment in your mother's eyes. The disappointment in yours or your brothers'. It was more than he could bear."

Lochlan clenched his teeth as each whispered word pounded him like a hammer through his heart. He desperately wanted to cry for the brother he'd loved so much. For the brother he'd hoped to find again.

But he was among strangers and that alone kept him stoic on the outside. Inside however, he was screaming out in pain again . . . just as he'd done the day when he'd found Kieran's sword and plaid by the loch.

And once again, he'd have to face his mother with the bitter news that her son was dead. It was the last thing he wanted to do, but as Catarina had said, he wasn't a coward and it wasn't the kind of news that should come from anyone save family.

"Thank you," Lochlan said past the lump in his throat, "for trying to save him. For being with him when I couldn't be."

Duncan turned toward him then and when their gazes met, Lochlan realized that they did share a bond in blood and in Kieran's love.

His gaze was blurry from his unshed tears as Lochlan held his hand out to this new brother. "I understand why you hate me, but should you ever need anything, send word and I will come."

Duncan stared at his hand for several heartbeats before he took it and pulled Lochlan into his embrace. "He loved you, Lochlan. I hated how much you meant to him. How much all of you did. I knew I was only half as good in his eyes. At least that's what I thought until he died for me. Then it was too late . . . it should never be too late for such things."

Lochlan clapped him on the back as his own anguish choked him. "Half or full blood makes no never mind to us. A brother is always a brother."

Duncan buried his hand in Lochlan's hair before he pulled him back and placed his forehead against Lochlan's. Grimacing, he pushed himself

Page 310

away and headed for the door. "You can rest here, if you like." He raised the cowl on his cloak.

"Raziel," he growled as he paused just before the door. "I've had enough of company. I want no more of it. Do not disturb me any more this night."

Lochlan took a step toward him, but Raziel cut him off as Duncan made his way out of the room.

"Press him no more," he said in a low, guttural tone. "It physically hurts him to talk and it hurts him even more to move. He must rest now and he never wants anyone to see him in that kind of misery. I beg you to allow him the dignity he deserves."

Lochlan wanted more answers, but he understood what Raziel was saying. "You don't seem like a servant to me. Why do you obey him so?"

"Duncan gave up his face for me when I was nothing but a worthless dog. There is nothing I wouldn't do for him now."

"Raziel is also one of the very few he trusts," Kestrel said quietly. He shook his head. "So it was Duncan who survived. Now we know for sure."

Catarina frowned. "I don't understand. How did Kieran know of him as a brother when you didn't?"

Lochlan had no idea.

"He was raised in a neighboring village," Raziel said. "His mother kept him hidden out of fear. She saw the way the lairdess treated her husband's bastards and so she sought to protect him as best she could. Unfortunately, she died when Duncan was only eight and he was left to struggle on his own. He met Kieran by accident a few years later and Kieran recognized him as a brother immediately. So he would take food and clothing to Duncan. Sometimes even coin. It was Kieran who bought him an apprenticeship with the local blacksmith."

Lochlan cursed as he remembered Kieran being caught stealing by their father. He'd never explained to anyone why he'd been doing it.

Now he understood. Kieran had been taking supplies for their brother.

"Why didn't he tell me?" Lochlan breathed.

"Duncan didn't want him to. He never wanted anyone to know he existed."

"Yet he went to Outremer with Kieran."

Raziel nodded. "He found Kieran on the bank of the loch, weeping. Kieran told him that he couldn't go home again. It was then they decided that they'd find their brother Sin and make their own family where no one would be more related than the other. Where there would never be harsh words or hurt feelings between them."

Those words cut Lochlan to the soul. "I never carried a grudge against any of my brothers."

Kestrel cast a look to Raziel, then to Lochlan. "It's far easier to give forgiveness than it is to ask for it."

Lochlan nodded. It was true. Kieran would have been too embarrassed over his tirade and actions to reach out to them and apologize. "I can't believe he's dead."

"I'm sorry, Lochlan," Catarina whispered.

He pulled Catarina against him. For the first time, his brother's death was almost tolerable.

Almost.

Raziel stepped forward. "I'm sure all of you are tired from your journey. Come with me and I'll show you to rooms where you may rest. Would you like for me to bring you food?"

Lochlan nodded. "A light repast for the lady. I know she has to be starving."

Kestrel cleared his throat. "And I'm most certain the two of them will be wanting a room together."

"That would be most improper," Lochlan said quickly.

Kestrel rolled his eyes. "Then for the love of God fetch a priest and marry her already."

Raziel looked horrified by the mere thought. "That would prove to be most difficult. The Scot refuses to have anyone of holy cloth near his home. His belief is that God turned His back on him and as such he will never welcome a cleric here again."

Kestrel scowled. "Not even Christian of Acre?"

"As a Brotherhood member, he's an exception and not a real priest, I might add."

"Well, there is that," Kestrel said. "But it doesn't usually stop him from wearing the robes."

Ignoring that, Raziel took them down the hall to a large bedchamber. When Lochlan started to withdraw and leave it for Catarina, Raziel took his arm. "No one here will judge you. We know how fragile and fleeting life is. Find your comfort where and when you can and trust we'll never breathe a word of it."

Lochlan knew he should leave, but honestly it was the last thing he wanted to do and he was grateful that Raziel understood that. "Thank you."

Raziel inclined his head to him before he shut the door and walked off with Kestrel by his side.

Cat watched Lochlan's uncertainty as he turned toward her and couldn't help smiling over it. Only he would be worried over her reputation after all they'd shared. It was endearing and sweet.

"We'll find that priest, Lochlan. Have no fear."

He nodded as he unbuckled his sword and set it aside. His silence concerned her. He was hurting.

Going to him, she wrapped her arms about his waist. "Your brother loved you."

She saw the tears return to his eyes and yet somehow he managed to keep them in check.

"I keep seeing him as a child," he said in a quiet tone. "He used to be the devil of a prankster. Putting burrs under my saddle or in my boots. One time he woke me in the middle of the night by telling me the castle was on fire. I went running outside completely naked only to have him laugh and wake half the castle to witness my horror."

Cat tried not laugh, but it was hard. "And still you loved him."

"More than my life. God, Catarina, we were to grow old together with me having to look under my saddle even in my winter years. How can he have died on foreign soil with strangers around him?"

"He had Duncan."

The anguish in his eyes stole her breath. "He should have had me. *I* was the older brother. 'Twas my job always to look after him. How could I have failed him so badly?"

"You didn't fail him, Lochlan. You loved him. There was nothing more you could have done."

Lochlan nodded. In his heart, he knew she was right, but the ache inside him denied it. It wanted his brother back and no amount of reason would make the pain or the guilt go away.

His heart breaking, he pulled her to his lips and kissed her with every part of himself. Right now, he needed her in a way he'd never needed anything. She kept the pain away. Made him glad he was still alive.

Wanting the salvation only she could give him, he scooped her up in his arms and carried her to bed.

Cat closed her eyes at the sensation of him holding her. Nothing felt better than being in Lochlan's arms. Nothing. The way he carried her, protective yet gentle, reminded her of how much he loved her. And she loved him with every part of her being. She wanted to kiss away every ounce of pain he'd ever endured. To satisfy him in a way no woman ever had.

He'd done everything he could for Kieren, she knew that. Deep down, Lochlan did, too. Sooner or later, he would forgive himself.

She hoped.

Gently, he placed her on the bed. Lochlan's gaze

met hers, intense and vulnerable in a way she'd never seen before. She could tell this was more to him than just coupling. He needed her and that touched her in a way nothing ever had before.

Lochlan wanted to forget all he'd just learned and she wanted to make him forget. He deserved so much more than the burdens he'd shouldered all these years. He deserved happiness, laughter, and love beyond his imagination. And she planned on giving that to him starting right now. Wearing an inviting smile, Catarina lifted his tunic over his head and allowed it to drop to the floor.

Her fingers itched to touch that hard, corded chest. He was a powerful man and a gentle, caring person all rolled into one. God, how she loved him.

"Kiss me." His tone was ragged with need.

She complied as his lips teased hers open. The way his lips moved over hers, it was as if they were the only two people in the world and she felt more love than she knew existed.

He stroked her cheek with the pad of his thumb. Without his uttering a single word, she knew. The pain was gone for a moment and she'd done that for him. Right now, he wasn't thinking of his brother.

He was only thinking of them.

Cat lifted a finger to his cheek so that she could scratch the stubble playfully with her nails. How she loved that sensation. His skin was so different from hers. So rugged and masculine.

Her mouth watered for a taste of it.

"You know, my lord, what with all that has happened, it seems you've forgotten to shave. 'Tis getting a little long for my priggish lord."

He leaned in and nuzzled her neck so that his stubble teased her skin, making chills run the length of her. "Is it? I thought you preferred me as wild and untamed as you are."

She couldn't help but laugh. "It isn't without its charms, but there is so much more I find charming about you, Lochlan MacAllister."

He nuzzled again and leaned in, pausing just shy of her ear. "And I find many, many more things about you irresistible."

"Such as?"

His eyes twinkled as he stared down at her. "Your earlobes."

She frowned at his response. What could he possibly find endearing about that? "My earlobes?"

"Aye, they're so tiny and delicate." He kissed her earlobe, the warmth of his breath sending a shudder down her spine.

"So you love me for my earlobes?"

He smiled. "Among other things."

"Other things?"

He traced the curve of her neck with his forefinger just before his lips followed. "Here." He sprinkled kisses down her neck, tender and loving. "I adore the way your neck curves. 'Tis most inviting."

"Mmm," she breathed. "And is there anything else you find inviting?"

Lochlan savored her playfulness now more than ever. She was trying to distract him and God love her, it was working. He was lost to her charm. Lost to the feel of her softness. "Aye, love, I do have a favorite."

Cat arched a brow at him. "Is that so?" She had an idea where his hand would travel next.

At least that was what she thought until it went somewhere else.

"Here." He placed his hand over her heart as his gaze captured hers. "This is the most beautiful part of you, Catarina. It is what holds me as your most willing captive."

That unexpected gesture stole her breath and brought a tear to her eyes. Overwhelmed by his tenderness, she cupped his face in her hands and pulled him into a deep kiss.

Lochlan trembled at the taste of her unbridled

passion. Something about his Catarina caused the agony he'd felt for Kieran to subside.

In this moment, he wasn't the MacAllister, a man who served his family and with no reservations and no future of his own. He was only the lucky bastard Catarina loved and that was enough for him.

Their kiss deepened and he slid his tongue into her mouth, teasing her, begging for compliance and solace. Forgiveness and hope. A comfort he found only here in her arms. In her bed. It was where the entire world melted away and there were only the two of them.

They kissed and explored one another for what seemed like forever. He ached to possess her, to sink himself so deep within her flesh that he'd lose all sense of reality. But he wanted to prolong this time with her. To savor it.

Then she broke the kiss.

"What's wrong?"

She looked at him with a hunger so raw it took his breath. "I want you inside me, Lochlan. I fear I'm going to burn to cinders if I don't have you there."

Her words brought a smile to his face. This wasn't a woman seducing the MacAllister in hopes of landing him as her husband. This was a woman who wanted him as a man.

And it was the most sensuous thing he'd ever known. His heart pounding, he quickly unlaced her gown and pulled it from her body. He sucked his breath in at the sight of her lying on the bed, fully exposed to him.

He jerked his boots and breeches off while she kicked her shoes away. His body on fire, he cupped her right breast in his hand, toying with the tip until she was groaning in pleasure. And then he did it all over again just to watch her writhing from his touch.

She closed her eyes and laid her head back onto the pillow. Unable to stand not tasting her, he bent down to take her soft nipple into his mouth.

Catarina cried out in pleasure as he flicked his tongue over the sensitive area. Desire pooled between her thighs and if she didn't have him soon, she feared she might very well die.

Yet there was no mercy in his eyes as he moved his hand to her ankle, tracing a path along her inner thigh to stop at the sensitive flesh where she desired him most. He slid a finger inside her with ease. She opened her legs wide, giving him more access as he toyed with her.

But that wasn't really what she wanted. It was merely a temporary relief of what she hungered for.

Unable to stand it, she reached down between their bodies to touch him. He growled as she stroked his cock. Laughing in triumph, she bucked his hand away and guided him into her body.

Lochlan wanted to curse from the biting ecstasy that tore through him. Being inside Catarina was heaven, pure and simple. The way she fit perfectly around him, her body so receiving. He thrust his hips against hers, moving in and out, savoring every movement of their joined bodies.

"Have you any idea what you do to me, lass?" he breathed in her ear.

She nibbled at his jaw. "I have a pretty good idea."

"Aye?"

"Aye," she said with a mischievous glint in her eye. "The very same thing you do to me." She cupped his face in her hands and pulled him into a kiss.

Something swelled inside Lochlan as he tasted the depth of her mouth and of her affection for him.

It was hope, he realized. She gave him hope in the most desolate of situations. Without her these last few days, he wasn't sure if he'd have even been able to make it.

He pressed himself deeper inside her. Losing

himself with each thrust as she held tight to him, whispering declarations of love into his ear as he grew harder and harder, but he would not have pleasure until he knew she was fully satisfied.

Holding back as much as possible, Lochlan lifted her thighs so he could slid farther inside her. She gasped as he filled her completely. It gave him great satisfaction to hear the little moans escape her mouth when he moved inside her. She belonged to him. He made her feel like this. Pride welled inside his chest at the thought.

And then she exploded around him, pulling and tugging at his back as she almost screamed his name. It was more than he could stand. Hearing his name from her lips sent him over the precipice. His release came so swiftly and deeply that it shook him all the way to his soul.

Sweaty and exhausted, he collapsed into the safety of her arms.

Cat bit her lip to keep from protesting his sudden weight. Aye he was heavy against her, but honestly, she'd have it no other way. More than that, she could still feel him inside her. She didn't know why that made her so possessive of him, but it did. This was the only man she'd ever love. She knew it.

And she didn't want to share him with anyone else.

"I'm crushing you, aren't I?"

She pouted up at him. "A little."

He nipped at her lips before he slid from her and rolled to his side. He tucked one arm behind his head before he stretched like a powerful lion. Cat savored the sight of his bared chest and the beauty that was him. Biting her lip to keep from moaning, she snuggled in beside him and closed her eyes.

Before she realized it, she was sound asleep.

Lochlan lay in the silence of the late-night hour, listening to Catarina's soft snore. It was so strange and surreal to have his quest settled after all this time. A part of him couldn't believe this was it.

It was really over.

When he'd started out, he'd expected to find his brother. What he'd never thought to find was the treasure that slept beside him now.

Would you trade this to have Kieran back?

It was a choice he was grateful he didn't have to make. But in the end, he knew the truth.

Catarina was his life. He would sacrifice anything for her.

Anyone.

And that honestly terrified him. No single person had ever held so much power over him. No one. The sad thing was, she hadn't even meant to take his heart. Somehow over the last few days, she'd worn her way past his resistance and given a gift that he'd never expected to receive.

Smiling at the first real happiness he'd ever known, he closed his eyes to sleep.

But the instant he did, he heard a sudden cry from outside.

"Open the damn door now or so help me, I'll pull this castle down stone by stone!"

"And who are you to make such a demand?"

"Philip Capet. King of France and father of the woman you harbor without my permission within your walls."

Chapter 16

There were some things that no man wanted to hear under any circumstance. One, that he'd lost his testicles in battle. Two, that he'd lost his testicles to a fluke injury. Three, that he'd caught some disease that interfered with his ability to perform as a man.

And most of all four, that the father of the woman, who was one of the most powerful men in all of Christendom, was at the gate of the home where he'd just violated the man's daughter without the sanctity of marriage. Four was guaranteed to cost him not just his testicles, but the rest of his internal organs as the king ordered them scraped from inside him while he was still alive enough to feel it.

I am dead. Disemboweled. Hanged. And, most unfortunately, not in that order.

He heard the men outside scrambling to obey the king's orders to open the gate to him. There was no easy way to start this day or to notify Catarina that the noose had suddenly fallen around their necks.

"Catarina?" he whispered, jostling her awake. "Lass, wake yourself."

She blinked open her eyes before she yawned. "Is it morning already?"

"Nay, lass," he said, wishing that was why he was waking her. "Your father is at the gate and will be here at any moment."

She shrieked indignantly as she jerked up so quickly that she almost pulled her hair out since a portion of it was trapped beneath his body. Lochlan grimaced in sympathetic pain before he lifted himself from her hair to free her.

There was a loud commotion outside as more shouts were exchanged. She gathered the sheet around her before she scrambled to the window to peer outside.

Lochlan hurriedly dressed. If he was going to

have to be gelded, he wasn't about to make it easy on them.

Her eyes panicked, Catarina turned back to face him. "How did he find us?"

He wasn't sure, but he had his theories. "Either he tortured Stryder until he broke under the stress or his informant was smarter than we gave him credit for."

Catarina tossed her hair over her shoulder as she looked about the room as if seeking an escape. "What am I going to do?"

He had no answer for that.

She looked about expectantly. "I'll bet there's an escape route from here. Someplace. The Scot is too paranoid for there not to be."

But even as that same thought went through him, he squelched it as reality sank in. "Is this really what we want?"

"What do you mean?"

He gestured toward the window. "Running constantly from your father for the rest of our lives?"

By her face, he could tell she was more than willing to continue this game. "Is this not what we agreed to?"

It was and yet now that they were virtually face-to-face with Philip, Lochlan didn't have it in him to run like a coward in the night.

Nay, he wasn't a thief or a criminal who had to slink away in fear of what he'd done. He was a grown man who'd been with the woman he loved. There was no crime in that. No harm.

He looked at Catarina. Aye, he'd taken something that didn't belong to him. But it didn't belong to Philip either. Catarina was her own person.

And it was time her father was made to see that.

"I'm going to speak with him."

She scowled. "Are you insane?"

Most likely. Only a fool would even contemplate this. And yet it seemed like the only decent thing to do. In spite of his own father's faults, he hadn't raised him to run from his problems. Lochlan had been trained from birth to stand his ground and defend what was important to him.

Nothing was more important to him than Catarina.

And he would go down fighting for her.

"Get dressed and be ready to run in the event my plan fails."

Suspicion clouded her dark eyes. "Are you coming with me?"

God willing. But he didn't want her to know exactly how uncertain he was over the outcome.

"Aye. But I owe it to us to at least attempt to speak to your father before we run off."

Cat wanted to scream at him for his blind stupidity. Her father wouldn't listen. He never listened. All that mattered to him was what *he* wanted. The rest of the world could be damned.

But she loved Lochlan and she knew this was what he needed to do. He wouldn't be able to live with himself unless he tried to negotiate a settlement with her father.

"If you get yourself killed, Lochlan MacAllister, so help me, I will *never* forgive you."

"Have no fear. I assure you, I shall have issues with myself over it."

She made a disgusted sound in the back of her throat. "Don't make light of this."

"I'm not, lass. Believe me, I more than understand the consequences of facing that man."

She pulled him against her and kissed him. "God keep you and make sure you can run fast if He doesn't."

Lochlan nuzzled her neck before he forced himself to break away from her. He glanced to his sword, then thought better of it. There was no need to provoke the king any further. This was a time of peace.

It's a time to run, you cursed moron.

Nay! It was the time to face her father like a man and make him understand that Catarina deserved something more than the milksop awaiting her.

"What kind of godforsaken hell have we come to?"

Lochlan paused on the landing to look down and see Philip there with two of his dukes and a number of French guards. The regal bearing alone was enough to betray the king, but so did his bald head and extreme height. He literally towered over the men around him.

And while scanning the group, Lochlan's gaze was held transfixed by the executioner who accompanied the group. Dressed all in black, he even wore a black hood that obscured his face.

Obviously the king wasn't here to negotiate.

"Who is the lord of this place?" the king demanded.

Raziel entered the hall on the king's left and bowed before the king. "My lord is abed, Your Majesty. He regrets that he is unable to join you."

The king arched a disdainful brow. "Unable?"

"He is a war hero, sire," Lochlan said aloud from his place on the landing.

The king's dark gaze swung up to him and it narrowed dangerously.

Lochlan forced himself to bow down to Philip.

"And who are you?"

"Laird Lochlan MacAllister, Your Majesty."

"You!" he snarled, as if Lochlan were the vilest of creatures. "You dare to show yourself to us?"

Lochlan knew it was dangerous to taunt the king, but still he couldn't resist playing ignorant. "Your Majesty has issue with me?"

"Of course we do. You took our daughter—"

"He protected me, Father. Those men you sent had beaten me and threatened me. Lord Lochlan should be commended for keeping me safe while the very ones you sent were out to do me harm."

Lochlan cut a sharp glare at Catarina, who had silently joined him. She was dressed in her pale gown with her hair left to tumble in curls around her shoulders.

"What are you doing?" he asked her in a low tone.

"What you've taught me to do, Lochlan. Stand my ground."

"Catarina . . ." he said from between clenched teeth.

She touched him gently on the face. "You were right. For better or worse, he is my father. I can't run from him for the rest of my life. 'Tis time I faced him as his daughter."

She left him to descend the stairs to where her

father waited. "I'm not a fox to be run to ground by your hounds, Father. And I tire of this game we play with one another."

"Then you've come to your senses?"

"If by that you mean I'm willing to marry your prince, nay. Never. I will not have him for husband and I will not be used as a pawn in your political games."

"You willful—"

"Stubborn, obnoxious child," she finished for him. "I know, Father. I am your bane. Your curse."

"But above all, she is your child, sire."

Cat turned to find Lochlan standing just behind her.

"Your insolence is not endearing you to us, boy."

Lochlan inclined his head to her father. "Forgive me, Majesty. But I'm not sworn to protect France. I'm sworn to protect Catarina from any who would do her harm."

Her father's face hardened instantly. "Do you understand the line you are crossing?"

Lochlan nodded. "Aye, Majesty."

"And you are willing to give your life for hers?"

She exchanged a scowl with Lochlan. "What say you?"

He jerked his chin toward his daughter. "Does her freedom mean more to you than your own life?"

Lochlan frowned at his question. Was he asking what he thought?

"Answer me, boy. Will you die for her freedom?"

Aye, he was indeed.

"Nay!" Cat shouted.

But Lochlan knew the truth and he didn't hesitate with the answer. "Aye, Majesty."

The king scoffed. "Words are ever easy to come by. 'Tis actions we respect." He snapped his fingers and the executioner came forward with his sword. "If you mean what you say, then kneel before us and let us sever your head from your body. The moment you die, her freedom from our will is granted."

Cat shrieked and would have clawed her father had one of his guards not seized her. "You rotten bastard! Damn you for this! Damn you!"

But there was no mercy on Philip's face.

Lochlan took a deep breath as he considered all he was giving up for her. But in the end, he knew it would be worth it. "I have your word that she will be free to roam as she pleases?"

"Absolutely. Bought and paid for in your blood."

Lochlan nodded before he turned to where Cat was fighting the guard with everything she had. "May I have a final moment with her, Majesty?"

He let out a disgusted breath. "We suppose a last request would not be unseemly given the circumstances."

Lochlan approached her slowly. "Catarina!" he snapped.

She stopped her fighting to look at him. Tears were streaming down her face as sobs racked her body. "Don't you do this, Lochlan. Don't you dare!"

His own eyes were misty as he used the sleeve of his tunic to wipe the tears from her face. She was so beautiful. So wonderful. "I told you, lass. One hour or a million. 'Tis enough for me."

"I can't lose you. Do you understand?"

He cupped her face in his hands as he tried to make her understand what she was gaining. "You will live and you won't have to run ever again. There will be no more looking over your shoulder. No more fear of being taken when you sleep. It's a small price I gladly pay for you."

She kicked her guard so hard, he released her so that she could run to him.

Lochlan scooped her up in his arms and held her close to him one last time.

"Why didn't you run with me when I asked you to?"

Lochlan had to bite back his own tears. "I wish I had, lass. Kestrel was right. It's what you don't do that haunts you most. I'm sorry. If I could go back to last night, I'd gladly run and forget everything else in the world."

Unable to stand it any longer, he brushed his lips over her cheek and inhaled the sweet scent of her skin. That was all he would take with him to his death. The memory of her touch. Of her scent.

He pushed her gently toward Raziel. "Don't let her see it."

Raziel nodded grimly as Catarina cried out in denial and reached for him.

Lochlan let her go and turned back to Philip, who was watching them with a stoic expression. This was the hardest thing Lochlan had ever done.

Run you bastard, run.

But he couldn't. He'd given his word and he would abide by that.

So he met her father's gaze levelly. Without fear or remorse. Well the latter most certainly wasn't true. He had remorse for every day he wouldn't live on this earth with Catarina.

Steeling himself, he dropped to his knees and lowered his head.

Cat fought against Raziel's hold. "Let me go!"

"Stop it!" Raziel hissed in her ear. "The man goes to his grave for you, woman. The least you could do is let him die without hearing your anguished cries ringing in his ears."

He was right and it was killing her. Lochlan deserved more than this.

"I love you, Lochlan," she said, hating the fact that her voice broke as she spoke the words. "I will always love you and you alone."

Raziel turned her toward the wall and held her so that she couldn't see what was happening.

"Have you any last words?" her father demanded of Lochlan.

Lochlan pulled the small crucifix from his neck. He crossed himself, then kissed it and held it out toward the king. "For Catarina." He glanced over his shoulder to see her cringing while trying to remain brave. "I love you, too, lass. May God keep you always."

Philip snatched the cross from his hand, then nodded to his executioner.

Lochlan braced himself for the blow. He saw the shadow of the man raising the sword on the stone floor. Closing his eyes, he prayed.

* * *

Cat heard the soft thunk behind her. And there in the firelight of the rising sun she felt her legs give away as the most unimaginable pain tore through her. She wanted to scream, but no sound could squeak past the vicious, burning lump of agony in her throat.

Lochlan was dead and it was all her fault.

She was only vaguely aware of Raziel holding her up. "I want to die, too," she whispered. "Please."

"Whatever happens in your life, girl," her father said from beside her, "I want you to remember this pain that you feel right now. Keep it close to your heart because so long as you remember it, it will keep you from being stupid again."

She looked up aghast at her father's cruelty.

Only it wasn't her father's face she saw, it was Lochlan.

He was alive and he was holding her.

"Wha . . . ?" It was a ridiculous response, but her mind couldn't grasp the fact that it was his arms holding her and not Raziel's. And he looked every bit as baffled as she felt. "I don't understand."

Her father narrowed his gaze on her. "You are a princess related to three monarchies, Catarina. Did you really think we would allow you to run away with someone who saw you as nothing more than a title?"

He looked at Lochlan. "Lord Stryder told us you loved her more than your life. But we didn't believe him. We needed to see proof of this love. Now we know exactly how far you are willing to go to ensure not just her life, but her happiness." For the first time, his features softened. "There is no better gift a father could have for his child."

Still Cat wasn't ready to forgive him quite so easily. "You insensitive beast!" she snarled as tears washed down her face. "This was so cruel."

He nodded. "In time I trust you will learn to forgive me. In the meantime, I have a priest outside who is willing to make an honest woman of you."

"What?"

Philip shrugged. "He was to either marry the two of you or perform Last Rites if Lochlan didn't agree to die for you."

Cat looked over her shoulder to see Lochlan's own baffled expression.

Before either of them could respond, the executioner threw off his cloak to reveal Stryder, who was smiling at them. "I suppose you should hate me, too. But trust me, I knew if the king saw for himself what was so obvious to the rest of us, he would never be able to condemn you to marry another."

Philip cleared his throat. "So are we going to have a wedding, or are we all going to stand around looking irritable?"

For the first time since Lochlan had shaken her awake, Cat allowed herself to smile. "Oh we're going to have a wedding, Father, and then you and I are going to have a long talk about mutual respect and about how you will never again do such a thing to me."

"Aye, but look to the bright side, child. When a man is knighted, he's given a stiff blow so that he'll always remember the moment. This was your blow to let you know exactly how much your husband means to you and how much he loves you. Everyone should be so blessed."

And in that moment, she realized he was right. Shaking her head, she left Lochlan's arms to stand before her father. "I may not always agree with your methods, but I do love you, Father. And I'm glad you came to your senses."

He laughed for an instant, then sobered. "Where's that priest? We want our daughter well settled."

Cat turned toward Lochlan and Stryder. "Trust me, Father. I couldn't be in better hands."

Epilogue

Six months later

Lochlan smiled as he left the kitchens with a loaf of fresh bread for Catarina. She was ripe with his child and craving hot bread. Far be it from him to deprive her of this even though it was almost midnight.

He still couldn't believe that she was his wife. Although the irritating presence of Bavel and Viktor in his home was more than enough to convince him that she was a permanent part of his life. Even so, she was worth the aggravation of their presence.

"Lochlan?"

He froze as he heard his name carried through the darkness on a light breeze. It was a voice he'd thought to never hear again.

His throat tightened. Surely, he was hearing things. "Kieran?"

A shadow to his right stirred.

He turned sharply, prepared to draw his sword. But as Kieran stepped out of the shadows and into the moonlight all he could do was gape.

It couldn't be . . .

"Is it really you?"

Kieran nodded.

"How is this possible?"

"There are some questions that should never be asked, brother. But I've heard you all these years, calling out to me . . . cursing me. Berating me." Kieran looked toward the castle. "I hear all of you and now that you have a chance for happiness, I didn't want to be the one thing that tainted it."

"But you're not dead."

"I am dead, Lochlan." Kieran opened his mouth to show him a set of fangs. "My soul was given up so that Duncan, Stryder, and the others could escape from our hell and do something good with their lives."

Lochlan didn't understand what had happened to

his brother, but if he'd given up his soul, there had to be some way to undo it. "We'll get your soul back."

"'Tis not possible. I made a bargain and I'm more than willing to abide by it. But I couldn't keep existing, knowing the pain I was causing you. I'm sorry for what I said to you, Lochlan. And I'm even more sorry for the pain I caused all of you. Please forgive me."

Kieran's presence here was unnatural and demonic. He knew it, but it didn't change the facts of their relationship.

"You're my brother, Kieran. How could I not forgive you?"

"Thank you." Kieran looked away and smiled. "Your wife needs you. She wants her bread and your son is eager to join this world."

"My son?"

"The babe is a boy. I can feel his soul. He's strong and good, like his father. Now I, too, must go." He stepped back, toward the shadows.

"Will I ever see you again?"

Kieran shook his head. "I'm forbidden to have contact with my family. But know that I hear you every time you think of me and tell Ewan to stop cursing me every time he sees water. It gets old." He smiled as if he heard Lochlan's thoughts. "I love you, too, brother."

And with that, Kieran vanished right before his eyes.

Lochlan stood there for several minutes, wondering if he'd dreamed it.

"*It wasn't a dream.*" Kieran's voice echoed in his head.

"Lochlan?"

He turned at the sound of Catarina's voice. "Aye, love. I was just coming."

She stopped on the short trail to scowl at him. "Are you all right?"

"Aye, I couldn't be any better."

"Good. I was talking to Bavel just now and we've decided on the baby's name should it be a boy."

"And that is?"

"Kieran, after your brother. Would you mind?"

Lochlan glanced back to where Kieran had appeared to him a moment ago. "Nay, love, I think that would be wonderful and I'm sure it will make my brother happy."

"And what of you?"

"So long as you are with me, lass, I can be nothing but delirious."

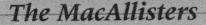